DAYS LIKE THESE

Meg is devastated when her husband, the unreliable Jamie, leaves her. But life goes on. She develops a friendship with a colleague, Robert. Then Meg makes the bittersweet discovery that she is pregnant with Jamie's child. When Jamie reappears, she can't bring herself to tell him he is to be a father — until it's too late . . . Baby James arrives, and Meg resolves to be as good a parent as she possibly can. But it's Robert, not Jamie, she misses . . .

MIRANDA BARNES

DAYS LIKE THESE

Complete and Unabridged

LINFORD
Leicester

British Library CIP Data

Barnes, Miranda
    Days like these.—Large print ed.—
Linford romance library
    1. Love stories
    2. Large type books
    I. Title
    823.9'2 [F]

    ISBN 978–1–84782–561–2

Published by
F. A. Thorpe (Publishing)
Anstey, Leicestershire

Set by Words & Graphics Ltd.
Anstey, Leicestershire
Printed and bound in Great Britain by
T. J. International Ltd., Padstow, Cornwall

This book is printed on acid-free paper

1

Meg would never forget the day Jamie left her. Nor the time. Nor what she was doing at the time. Everything was etched deeply in her memory and in her heart forever. As were his words, words so ordinary she scarcely noticed them at the time.

'I'm going now, Meg,' he said.

She turned from the cooker, casserole dish in her hands, and sighed with a mixture of exasperation and amusement.

'Going? Jamie you can't go now. For heaven's sake! This is just about ready, and they'll be here any minute now.'

He shrugged and said he was going anyway. He had to.

'Well, be quick. How long will you be?'

She assumed he wanted a quick pint or to buy a packet of cigarettes, even though he maintained he wasn't drinking much now and he'd given up smoking again.

'I'm going,' he repeated, for once not smiling. 'For good, I mean,' he added.

It was the missing smile that told her it was different this time. The words themselves had little meaning. Jamie's words seldom did. He just said what suited him, or suited his purposes. She knew that. It could even be endearing. But not when he didn't smile.

'Goodbye, Meg.'

'Jamie!'

But he was gone.

She was stunned. For a long moment, all she could do was stare at the empty doorway. Then the heat from the Pyrex dish burned through the thin part of one of the oven gloves. She dropped the dish on to the hob and in a panic rushed after him.

She reached the front door and wrestled it open, just in time to see Mike and Jenny climbing out of their car. But there was a gap, a hole in the world, where Jamie's car should have been.

'Hi, Meg!' Jenny called, waving the bunch of flowers she held in one hand.

Meg vaguely waved back, distracted, but her eyes went up and down the street. Where was he? How could he have disappeared so fast?

Of course! He must have parked the car round the back and gone out that way to avoid their visitors.

'How very nice of you to be here to welcome us,' Mike said, as he climbed the steps to the front door. 'How are you, Meg?' he added, planting a kiss on her cheek.

'Freesias,' Jenny said with a smile, thrusting the bouquet into her arms.

Meg, in a daze, stood aside and let them pass into the house. In the dim light, they hadn't noticed anything amiss. They hadn't even noticed that she hadn't spoken. Not one word. She was paralysed. She tried to open her mouth, and did manage it, but nothing came out. She was terrified.

She closed the door. She felt sick and panicky. She felt like screaming. She turned and, in a daze, followed her visitors through to the lounge.

'Something smells good!' Mike declared, sniffing appreciatively at the scents drifting in from the kitchen.

Meg, clutching the flowers, sagged against the wall and stared emptily into space.

'I'll put them in water,' Jenny said, reclaiming the freesias.

'So where's himself?' Mike asked, as he sank heavily into the sofa. 'Not back yet? Working late?'

Meg stared at him. She couldn't think of anything to say. Her heart was jumping. She was sweating heavily.

'I turned the gas off,' Jenny announced, coming back into the room. 'But your casserole looks done to me.'

She looked troubled now. She stood staring at Meg, who suddenly pressed her face into her hands.

'Oh, Meg! What's wrong?' Jenny cried, reaching out to wrap her arms

4

around her. 'What is it? Where's Jamie?'

Suddenly it was very quiet in the room. Meg knew it was her turn to say something. Anything. 'He's gone,' she mumbled, avoiding Jenny's anxious eyes.

'Gone? Where to?' Mike demanded. 'The sly so-and-so! Without me, as well. *The Queen's Head* or *The Packhorse*? I'll go and roust him.'

'Shut up, Mike!' Jenny warned, sensing a different scenario.

Mike grimaced.

'Have you two had a row?' Jenny asked.

Meg shook her head.

'What's the matter, then?'

'He's left me,' Meg whispered through tear-blurred eyes.

'Left you? When?'

'Five minutes ago — just before you arrived.'

'Dear God!' Jenny said, shocked.

'When he knew we were coming?' Mike asked indignantly.

He began to say something else but

shut up when Jenny flashed him a look of pure anger.

It had all happened in such a pitifully short time, and the enormity of it finally overwhelmed Meg's defences. Tears flowed. She began to sob uncontrollably, no longer caring what her guests thought.

2

The next day Meg went to work as usual, because in the end she could think of nothing else to do. She was exhausted, totally washed out, but she needed the comfort of purpose and routine. And she couldn't be on her own. She couldn't bear that.

Jenny and Mike had eventually left the previous night, but she had no idea when. She couldn't remember what they had done or said during the evening, or even if they had had dinner.

The bus was crowded, as usual. But she managed to grab a seat as someone stood up to get off. She slumped into it gratefully. When she had caught her breath, she raised a hand and wiped away a little patch of condensation from the window beside her.

Then she peered out at the crowded pavement, almost as if she hoped to see

Jamie there, even though she knew he wouldn't be. He would be driving. In his car, at least. Wherever he was, he would be in his car or it would be nearby. The red BMW was his pride and joy, his most-loved possession. More loved than her, anyway. Obviously.

She shivered. He hadn't come home last night. She'd waited and waited. She'd been going to tell him it didn't matter that he'd upset her. She forgave him. It didn't matter that he'd missed Mike and Jenny either. They would get over it. Or not. It didn't matter. It just didn't matter.

She would have told him all that. Then they would have smiled at each other ruefully. She knew Jamie, what he was like. She ought to. Five years now, they'd been together. Three years married.

But he hadn't come home. He hadn't come back at all. Now she didn't know what to think, or to do. Except go to work, like she always did.

The office was hot. You could almost see steam rising from the plant pots on the window ledge. She liked that. Heat made her feel good. Better, anyway.

But Robert didn't like heat. Robert was an outdoors type. So he was always there early. And he opened all the windows, to let out as much heat as possible before the others arrived and demanded that he shut them. He was a nuisance. Selfish, too. But he was the boss, the Section Head at least.

She sometimes wished she worked in an all-female office. Then the windows would stay shut. There wouldn't be this constant battle between Robert and the other three men and the six women in the section.

'Morning, Meg!' Robert called, looking up with surprise. 'You're early, aren't you?'

'Am I?'

She knew she was. Of course she was. She'd been up all night, hadn't she?

'God, you look rough!' he added with a cheerful grin.

'Thank you,' she said. 'And good morning to you, too, Robert.'

Doing her best to be normal, to appear as normal as she could do. It was the only way.

She sat down at her desk and switched on the computer. She didn't care what time it was. She didn't care if she looked rough or not. She didn't care what Robert thought either.

She liked her job well enough but she didn't like everyone who worked in the Civic Centre. Why should she? And Robert was one of those she didn't much care for, although she couldn't really say she positively disliked him. She just had very little in common with him, and even less interest in him.

He was thirty-five, probably. Besides, he was a cold fish. No-one knew much about Robert. He wasn't the sort of man to talk about anything other than work.

The machine hurried through its warm-up phase. The screen flickered and came to life, and was suddenly ready with its *Welcome to Morning!* message. Then the machine waited to be told what to do next.

The others drifted in one by one, taking advantage of the flexi-time system. Fiona was usually last, as she had twin boys to get to the nursery on her way to work, but not today.

'Mam's taking the boys,' she said. 'Isn't that great? I thought I might beat you for once, Meg. But here you are! It must be lovely to get up in the morning knowing all you have to do is get yourself to work. I can't remember what it's like. You won't be able to either once you and Jamie start a family.'

Meg managed a token smile, though she felt like putting her head on the keyboard and weeping.

★　★　★

Jamie didn't call in the first hour. Nor the second. Then it was coffee time, and Robert's turn to make it. The Section was very democratic.

'Black and no sugar, right?' he asked, collecting the mug from the edge of her desk.

'Thanks, Robert. Yes, that's right.'

He returned a couple of minutes later, with a tray of steaming mugs. 'Meg, I've got some paracetamol, if you would like a couple?' he said, as he handed over her mug.

'Paracetamol?' she repeated, staring at him with bemusement.

'I use them for headaches myself. These lights,' he added, glancing up at the fluorescent strips on the ceiling. 'They're famous for causing migraines, and what not.'

'Oh?'

'If you don't feel well,' he told her with an unexpected smile, 'just go on home. The job will still be here tomorrow. If there's anything urgent, let me know. I'll sort it out for you.'

He left her to it then, before she could protest that there was nothing wrong with her. But there was. Something deeply wrong. And it must be obvious, she though with despair, if even Robert had noticed.

Somehow she hung on, and got through to lunchtime. Then she disappeared out into the shops. One thing about working in the city centre, she thought with relief, was how many shops there were, and how crowded they were. You could just lose yourself.

How could he do this? She wondered miserably. How could he do it to her? Her vision blurred. She staggered and lurched sideways. Someone grabbed her arm.

'Are you all right, pet?' Her vision cleared. Her head stopped swimming. She realised she was seated on a bentwood chair.

She looked up into the face of an older woman who had one arm around her. The woman's eyes were worried, but she smiled now. Meg straightened up and let go of the counter she had been clutching.

'Thank you, yes,' she stammered. 'I nearly . . . '

'I know. It's the heat in here. You were nearly away there.'

She must have been about to faint, she realised. Perhaps she had? Lucky someone had noticed.

'I'll be all right now,' she said, beginning to get to her feet. 'Thank you.'

'You take care now. I know what it's like when you're carrying. I should do. I've had four of my own!'

The woman smiled. She seemed relieved that Meg had recovered.

'Oh, I'm not . . . '

'You get outside, pet, into the fresh air. It'll do you the world of good.'

The woman assumed she was pregnant, Meg thought with something like dismay. Well, she wasn't.

Satisfied, the woman left her. Meg took her advice and headed for one of the exits.

'All right?' Robert asked, glancing up as she hung her coat on the stand near her desk.

She nodded. 'Fine, thanks. By, it's

chilly out there!'

She hoped she sounded cheerful and normal. The way Robert was looking at her, though, she guessed she didn't. She'd better make more of an effort.

'How are the kids, Robert?'

'Dangerous.'

'Dangerous?'

'Loaded with germs. From school, and play school. Everything going, they pick up and bring home. They're like weapons of mass destruction. The only things they haven't got are typhoid, bubonic plague and loss of voice.

'Everything else they've got?'

'Or they've already had. Anything they've missed by some little quirk will be coming soon.'

'You do well to stay so healthy then.'

He smiled and said, 'Needs must. I'm slowing down, mind. There was a time when I'd have had these invoices sorted by this time on a Friday.'

'Can I give you a hand?' she asked, surprising herself.

He deliberated for a moment and

then said, 'Yeah, OK. If you've got time?'

She joined him and they spent half-an-hour sorting out the problem. Then she returned to her own desk.

Friday, she thought sadly. Oh, Jamie! What am I to do?

At three he called. 'Are you all right?' she asked.

'Yeah. Fine.'

'Where are you?'

'Meg, I just thought I'd better tell you I've been for my stuff. You haven't had a burglar, or something.'

'Stuff. What stuff?'

'Clothes and things.'

'Oh, Jamie! What's happening? You don't need to do that. What's wrong?'

'See you, Meg.'

'Where are you going?' she asked desperately.

'I'll let you know.'

'You can't mean this!'

'I do. I want out. So do you, really, if you're honest with yourself.'

'I don't. I . . . '

She stopped. He'd hung up.

She put the phone down and stared hard at the calendar on the pinboard in front of her. Tears were not far away.

'Bad news?' Carol enquired from a nearby desk.

Meg nodded without looking at her. She wondered if Carol had heard. She must have done. Part of it, at least.

It didn't matter. She didn't care. Nothing mattered now.

'Why don't you go home?' Carol suggested.

She shook her head. She couldn't do that. Home? She didn't have one now. There was a house, with her things in it. That was all. She was in no hurry to go there.

But she couldn't stay in the office either. She left at four, the earliest she could. While waiting for the lift, Robert joined her.

'That's another one over,' he said.

She nodded.

Then the lift came and they both pressed inside, the dozen people already

17

there reluctantly making way for them.

The pressure of bodies and faces was overpowering. Meg held her breath and closed her eyes. Jamie! She was thinking. Oh, Jamie!

'Meg?'

She opened her eyes. People were surging out of the lift. Robert was looking at her, his face and voice registering concern.

'You're not well, are you?'

She shook her head but said, 'I'll be all right.'

She moved unsteadily towards the door. Robert held her by the elbow, and steered her through the gap and out into the street. She was glad of the support.

Outside, it was bitterly cold now. It was very nearly dark and an east wind was blowing with sharp little gusts that sent the leaves left over from autumn spiralling into the January air,

'Come on,' Robert said. 'I'll run you home.'

'The bus . . . '

'Catch that another day, when you're feeling better.'

She hadn't the strength to object, or to think straight. Everything was a struggle.

Robert's car was in a nearby car park, just a couple of minutes' walk away.

'Costs a fortune, parking here,' he said, 'but I have to pay it. I need the car to be handy.'

'What about the Metro?'

He shook his head. 'That's all right for where I live, and where I work, but not for getting to the childminder's.'

'You're a busy man,' she said lightly, beginning to recover a little.

'You're telling me! But needs must.'

'Does your wife pick the children up some days?'

'Not really.'

She wondered what that meant. It wasn't a yes and it wasn't a no. He opened the passenger door and saw her inside. He was very gallant, she thought with reluctant appreciation, as he walked round to the driver's side.

'Gosforth, isn't it?' he asked, as he got in.

She nodded. 'Just off Salters Road.'

'Right. Let's see if we can beat the traffic.'

Too late, she thought of the children.

'What about the childminder?'

'She won't mind me being a few minutes late.'

'More than that, surely?'

'It doesn't happen often. Emergency, I'll tell her,' he added with a grin.

The traffic was heavy already. Driving wasn't easy in the evening rush, which seemed to start soon after lunch these days. Robert didn't say a lot, for which she was grateful. She closed her eyes and tried to wish a developing headache away. But wondering what she would find at home made it impossible.

Maybe Jamie would be there after all? Perhaps it had been a joke, or a mistake. He couldn't have been well last night. He liked Jenny and Mike. He wouldn't have wanted to miss them.

They were more his friends than hers anyway.

It was a forlorn hope. As soon as they turned into her street, she knew Jamie wasn't there. No red BMW. No lights on in the house. Her spirits, briefly raised by hope, sank again.

'Take care,' Robert said as he let her out of the car. 'Look after yourself, and try to have a good weekend.'

She gave him a weak smile and a little wave as he drove off. Then she fumbled for her key and headed for the front door.

The house was cold. The heating hadn't come on yet. And it was dark. After she had shut the front door, she stood still for a moment, almost afraid to go any farther. If she stayed where she was, she reasoned, everything might go back to how it had been.

But it didn't. She switched on the lights and went through to the kitchen to turn on the heating. Then she went upstairs, dreading what she would find.

She saw at a glance that Jamie really

had been and gone. She stared with dismay at the open and empty wardrobe that had housed his clothes. She opened a couple of his drawers. Empty, too, apart from bits of rubbish.

She stared. Then she flung herself on to the bed and began to weep. She wept until her insides, as well as her heart, ached.

3

On Saturday morning Meg was sitting in the kitchen staring at a cup of tea she had made but couldn't drink. She rushed to answer the doorbell, knowing it must be Jamie at last. He'd forgotten his key. Lost it again, more like.

'You needn't look so disappointed!' Jenny protested with a wry chuckle.

'I thought it was someone else.' She recovered. 'I mean, I thought . . . '

'I know what you thought. But it's only me. Can I come in?'

Meg stood aside reluctantly.

Jenny came in, closed the door and wrapped her arms around her. 'Any word?' she asked.

Meg shook her head. It was hard to hold back the tears.

'I'm so sorry,' Jenny said as they moved apart. 'How are you?'

Meg shrugged and turned to lead the

way into the kitchen.

'You've heard nothing?' Jenny said, following her.

'He called me at work, to say he'd been to collect his things. But that's all.'

Jenny gave a sad smile and walked over to put the kettle on. She was so competent, Meg thought dully, watching her. Nothing like this would ever happen to her.

'But what do you think?' Jenny asked.

Meg shook her head. 'I don't know,' she repeated miserably. 'I really don't know.'

'Was anything wrong? Have you been having problems?'

'No. Nothing was wrong. Nothing at all.'

'We did wonder, Mike and I. We seem to have seen Jamie about the town a lot lately.'

'Oh, he's always out and about. That's what he likes. He can't be stuck in the house all the time.'

'Without you, though?'

'I like to be at home. I'm too tired to be out every night.'

Jenny sipped her coffee thoughtfully. 'Had he been drinking more than usual?' she asked.

'Not really, no. He doesn't drink a lot anyway. Why?'

'Just wondered. Maybe he's having difficulties at work?'

'No, he isn't. He's selling more cars than ever.'

'Do you still love him?'

'Of course!' she said quickly. 'Don't be so silly.'

She could tell Jenny was thinking, if not actually asking, if Jamie still loved her. She didn't know the answer to that one. Until two days ago, she wouldn't have had any doubts at all. Now she didn't know.

'Let's go shopping?' Jenny suggested. 'See if we can find some shoes we like. You need to think about something else for a while.'

Meg shook her head. 'No,' she said firmly. 'I can't do that.'

'Lunch, then? That little pizza place round the corner?'

★ ★ ★

Gianni's was quiet for once. The place was still recovering from the night before. The waiters solemnly distributed dishes and plates as if they were part of a religious ceremony.

'He's gone for good, isn't he?' she said, surprising herself.

Jenny looked up from the menu.

'Jamie, I mean.'

Jenny squeezed her arm. 'I don't know, sweetheart. What did he say?'

'He said he was going for good.'

'Well, that's . . . ' Jenny paused. She had been going to say that was a pretty good clue. But she started again: 'It's too soon, Meg. He might just have been saying that. He'd had a bad day.'

'No.' Meg shook her head. 'He meant it. He's gone. What am I to do?'

'Have a glass of wine?'

They stared at one another until it sank in and became the funniest thing Meg had heard in a long time. Then she began to smile, to chuckle and finally to laugh out loud. 'Yes!' she said. 'A glass of wine. That's the answer!'

Come Monday morning, Meg went to work again. She was glad to get out of the house. No word from Jamie all the weekend, and by now she was beginning to tell herself she didn't care. She could manage. If necessary, she could live without him. She'd done it before. She could do it again.

'No Robert?' she asked Carol, who for once was early.

'Not yet.' Carol glanced at the clock on the wall and added, 'Perhaps he got a better offer.'

'What — on a Monday morning?'

Laughing, they got on with their work. For Meg, it was a relief. She'd spent enough time sitting and thinking, and wondering what was going to happen.

Robert arrived at ten, the very last moment allowed under the flexi-time system.

'Cutting it fine, Robert!' Carol called.

'The Tyne Bridge fell down,' Robert

27

explained. 'I had to wait till they got it back up again.'

Carol laughed and shook her head. 'That's a new one,' she said. 'I haven't heard that one before.'

Meg glanced across at him. He looked as if something had happened. Not bridge collapse, perhaps, but something. Hair all over the place. Shirt with a button missing. No tie. It wasn't like him to look so dishevelled. He must have been in a terrible hurry this morning. He caught her studying him and gave a little grimace. She smiled sympathetically.

Later, she went to see him about a report they were working on together.

'Good weekend?' he asked.

'Not really, no,' she said with a shrug. 'But I'm feeling better,' she added, to pre-empt his next question.

'Good.'

But Robert didn't look good, she thought. There were lines on his face and dark bags under his eyes that were not there normally.

'How about you?' she asked with some concern.

'I'm fine, thanks.' He smiled, making himself look even more ghastly. 'Come on! Let's get on with it.'

But he wasn't himself. She could see that. And his brain wasn't as sharp as it usually was either. The work was slow going.

'Meg!' Carol called, putting an end to her wondering. 'Phone call.'

She returned to her desk to take the call. It was Jamie. She thought she would fall apart when she heard his voice.

'Hi, Meg. How's it going? All right?'

'I . . . '

'Look, I haven't got much time. Can you do me a favour?'

'Jamie, what's . . . ?'

'When I was round the other day, I couldn't find my passport. Can you have a look for it? I need it. Just send it to the office.'

'I'll . . . '

'Thanks, Meg.'

The line began to buzz. He'd hung up, she realised. She was dumbstruck for a moment. Then she was furious with herself. She hadn't even said anything. Not one thing!

Passport? What did he want with that? She knew where it was, all right, but she wasn't sending him it. The cheeky so-and-so!

But how typical, she thought. How like Jamie.

They worked on till lunchtime. Then Robert suggested a sandwich in the staff restaurant.

'Good idea,' Meg said. 'I haven't brought anything today, and I'm starving.'

She got herself a salad, and a wholemeal bun to go with it. Robert went for mince and dumplings, and then spent most of the time playing with the food instead of eating it.

'You should eat,' she told him.

'Yeah.' He sighed, sat back and gave her a rueful smile. 'I'd rather just have a cup of coffee. What about you?'

'Tea, please.'

While he was away, she wondered what was on his mind. Something was bothering him. She could tell that. But it was his business.

When he returned with two coffees, she pretended she had wanted coffee all along. He slumped in his seat and refused to take the money for the drink.

'There's something on my mind,' he explained. 'You were right. I do have a problem.'

'Anything I can help with?'

'There's somewhere I have to be this evening, that's all. Something needs to be done.'

'And it's going to be difficult?'

'Maybe. But the main problem is the babysitter. The usual one said she can't make it, and we haven't found anyone else yet.'

They returned to the office and got through the rest of the work quickly. Robert pushed back his chair and rubbed his face with his hands. 'I'd better make some phone calls,' he said.

'About tonight?'

He nodded.

'Look, if you can't find anyone, let me know. I'm free tonight. I wouldn't mind sitting in for an hour or two.'

'Thanks, Meg,' he said with some surprise. 'I'm sure that won't be necessary, though.'

She was surprised herself. At least I offered, she thought later. That had seemed the least she could do, considering how kind Robert had been to her the other day.

Meanwhile, there was her own problem to worry about. What on earth was Jamie playing at? Had he found someone else? She wondered with a sinking feeling. Was that it?

Miserably, she concluded she still had no idea. And there was nothing she could do either, except wait.

'Are you sure you're not doing anything?'

She looked up. She hadn't noticed Robert approaching.

'Tonight?' he added apologetically. 'I

can't find a sitter.'

'No,' she said. 'I'm free tonight.'

And every other night, she thought bitterly.

'Would you . . . ?'

'Of course. No problem.'

'I really am grateful, Meg. Can you contact your husband to let him know?'

She wasn't sure what to say to that. It was far too complicated and delicate even to think of trying to explain.

'That's OK, Robert.'

'It's just that it's an early meeting. So it would be best if we could go straight to my place from here.'

'All right.'

'Sure?'

She nodded.

'Just one thing,' Robert added, looking slightly uncomfortable. 'There's just me and the kids.'

She nodded. Afterwards she wondered what was so strange about that.

4

The children were no trouble. After supper they got themselves ready for bed, more or less. But Kirsty needed a little help to put her pyjama bottoms on.

'It's 'cos of the 'lastic,' she declared.

'Yes, of course it is.' Meg laughed.

'You're not supposed to laugh at her,' Sean said from the doorway. 'She's only little. You're supposed to help her.'

Meg spun round with surprise, to see Sean, so solemn, standing with a toothbrush in his mouth.

'But she's so funny!' Meg protested. 'Just look at her now.'

Kirsty had wormed her way under the duvet and was busy wriggling her way to the bottom of the bed.

'Meg's helping me!' Kirsty yelled when she re-emerged. 'She's tucking me in.'

Sean seemed mollified. Meg smiled at him. Then she turned, lifted Kirsty up, gave her a hug, and returned her to the proper place in the bed.

'There!' she said. 'Now, do you want a story?'

'Yes, please.'

Meg read a few pages from a book that Kirsty said was her favourite. She would have gone on longer, but when she looked up she saw the little girl was already asleep.

She smiled and closed the book. How lovely she is, she thought wistfully, gazing down at the untroubled little face. Robert was so lucky to have her. To have Sean, too. They were lovely children. He seemed to be doing a good job with them, too. It couldn't be easy. Far from it.

It was obvious now what he'd meant when he said there was just him and the children. No wife and mother around. At all. That's what he'd meant.

She wondered what had happened. She had never heard anything in the office, and doubted if anyone there knew. Robert's secret. Looking after the children himself. Strange. Why had he kept it so quiet? Whatever 'it' was.

Well, why shouldn't he keep it quiet? She wasn't exactly broadcasting to the world the fact that Jamie had left her, was she?

Well, that was because he hadn't! Not really. Jamie hadn't left her. He couldn't have. He was just . . .

She blinked back tears. She didn't know what was happening. She would just have to wait and see.

She tiptoed out of the room and quietly closed the door after her. 'Don't shut it!' a voice behind her whispered fiercely. 'She doesn't like it to be closed. She gets scared.'

'Thank you, Sean. I didn't know that.'

She opened the door slightly and peeked in to satisfy herself that Kirsty hadn't woken up. When she turned round, Sean had disappeared back into his own room. She hovered on the landing, uncertain whether or not to look in on him. After all, Sean was eight.

'Meg!' she heard him call in a loud whisper. 'Will you read me a story, please?' he asked when she looked round the door.

She smiled at the solemn little face peering out from beneath the quilt. He was still only a little boy after all, even if he was long past three.

'What books have you got, Sean?'

He handed her a thick, battered paperback he took from the shelf above his bed.

'It's a big book,' she said dubiously, thinking she wouldn't be able to read him much of that even if she was here a month. '*Watership Down?* What's it about?'

'Rabbits,' he said quickly.

'Are you sure . . . ?'

'Yes,' he said quickly. 'Just a few pages.'

A marker stuck out a little past half-way.

'Has somebody else been reading this to you?' she asked, turning to the marked page.

'Yes,' he said. 'But not recently.'

She nodded and began to read, wondering, as she did so, who had left the page marker.

Sean fell asleep quickly, too. Meg carefully laid the book down on the bedside table. Then she picked it up again and opened the front cover. *Elizabeth Hardwick, Christmas* 1976, she read.

She had made herself a cup of coffee and was sipping it when she heard a key in the front door. She got up and looked into the hall in time to see Robert closing the door after him.

'Everything all right?' he asked quietly, seeing her waiting.

'Fine. No problems at all.'

She would have liked to ask how his evening had been, but didn't want to sound as if she was prying.

'I was just having a cup of coffee,' she said instead.

'I'll join you.'

Before she could say she would get it, Robert had grabbed the kettle. 'Well,' he said, sitting down on the other side of the table with a steaming mug. 'I can't hear them. So they must be asleep. Either that or they've gone out?'

'Asleep,' she chuckled. 'Kirsty first. Then Sean. I read to them but that didn't last long. They must have been tired.'

Robert nodded. 'Did they say anything? Tell you anything, I mean,' he added, as he saw the question forming on her lips.

She shrugged. 'They talked to me, but not in the way I imagine you mean.'

He rubbed his eyes with his hands. He looked more tired than ever. But he gave her a wry smlle. 'You must think I'm a worn-out old man!' he suggested.

She shook her head. 'I can see you're a very tired one, though, which is not surprising in the circumstances.'

'Circumstances? What circumstances?' he demanded brusquely, the smile gone completely.

She got up and collected her things, ready to leave.

'I'm sorry, Meg,' he said with a sigh. 'I didn't mean to sound rude. It's just that I'm exhausted, and I've had a very difficult evening.'

'That's all right. I'll be on my way now. It's getting late.'

'Yes. So it is. Thanks a lot for coming over. I don't know what I'd have done without you. I'll call a cab. I'd like to run you home, but I can't leave the kids alone.'

While they waited, Robert made an effort to bridge the gap that had developed between them. It was hard going. Meg was glad when the front door bell signalled the arrival of the taxi.

'You were right, by the way,' he said at last. 'I am on my own with them.'

'You told me that.'

'Liz, my wife, passed away a couple of years ago. It's been a struggle since then for us all.'

Meg was shocked. 'Oh, I'm so sorry,

Robert,' she said. 'I had no idea. No-one in the office has ever said . . . '

'They don't know.' He shrugged and added, 'I never said anything.'

She stared at him until the doorbell woke her up again. Then she grimaced and said, 'You really are doing very well. I admire you.'

'There's nothing much to admire. But I'm doing my best. Anyway, I thought you should know what the situation is. The least I could do, given that you've given up your evening.'

Doing his best? She thought as the taxi sped her home. It was a very good best. Suddenly her own problem seemed a small one in comparison.

5

Pregnant? I can't be!' Meg felt the colour draining from her face and her breath quickening.

Meg's GP, Dr Ella Armstrong, chuckled and said, 'If I had a pound for every time one of my patients has said that . . .'

Meg stared at her.

'You really didn't guess?'

'No. I . . .'

'No clues? No morning sickness, for example? No feeling dizzy?'

'Well, yes. But I thought . . . There are other things going on in my life. It didn't occur to me that this might be the reason.'

Dr Armstrong nodded and looked down at her notes. Meg could see she had limited time for, and interest, in non-medical things.

'Well, Meg. You're fit as a fiddle.

There's nothing wrong with you. So you and your baby should have a happy and interesting few months. Now I don't want to rush you but . . . You need to get along home and share your good news with your husband. He's going to be delighted, isn't he?'

Meg nodded non-committally. Jamie? Delighted?

She got up, but she had no idea what to do next.

At the end of the week she decided to visit her parents. They lived in a small village in Northumberland, near Alnwick. More a hamlet than a village, though it gloried in the name of Great Newton. It was a place she had been unable to wait to get away from when she was at school, but it was still her home. Whenever she returned, she felt that keenly. She even suspected she might return for good one day. But not just yet.

This time she was visiting because she simply couldn't bear the thought of another weekend on her own in the house, and because she had to talk to someone other than Jenny about what was going on.

Her mother hugged her as if she had been away a year, not a few weeks.

'Don't fuss, Mum!' Meg laughed.

'What do you expect? Of course I'm going to fuss! I haven't seen you for ages.'

They wandered into the big kitchen of Bracken Cottage. With its wood-burning stove, that had always been the centre of family life. Meg shivered with pleasure at the heat and gazed around appreciatively.

'And what about you, love? Any news?'

Meg shook her head. Not yet, she decided. She couldn't say anything yet. She didn't know where to start.

'Where's Dad?'

'Down the garden somewhere. Go and see if he wants to join us for a coffee.'

'If I can find him.'

'He'll be there. Where's Jamie, by the

way? Is he not with you?'

For a moment she almost said, No, he isn't. Not any longer. Not any more. Not at the moment, anyway. Then she shook her head and made for the back door, still unsure what, if anything, she wanted to say about Jamie.

She breathed in deeply as soon as she was outside, and paused to take stock. Bracken Cottage had been built in the early years of the nineteenth century, like so many of the local houses. Attractive, they were too, with their dressed stone walls and slate roofs. As ever, Meg couldn't help comparing them favourably with the cramped city streets where her life was lived now.

The garden was long and narrow. Originally, again, it had been one of the strips of land awarded to men who had served loyally in the Duke's own regiment during the Napoleonic Wars. Now, with its herbaceous borders, the vegetable plot and the fruit trees along the edges, it gave Meg's father ample scope for escape into the open air he loved.

She set off down the garden, following the new paving stones that not long ago had replaced the cinder path of her childhood. Inevitably, she smiled. Then she chuckled and shook her head. She only had to set foot in the garden for happy memories to come flooding back.

'Here you are, Dad!'

He looked up and turned towards her, and his face lit up with astonishment and delight at the sight of her.

'Meg? What a surprise! How are you, pet?'

'Fine, thanks. What about you? What are you up to?'

They grinned at each other. Then they stepped forward, to exchange hugs and kisses.

When they parted, her father gestured at the Leylandii hedge that helped keep marauding cattle and sheep out of the garden. Sunlight, as well.

'I'm just having a go at this little lot

46

before it gets completely out of control.'

'That'll look nice! Come on in and have a coffee with Mum and I before you start.'

He grinned, laughed out loud and started shepherding her back towards the house.

She told them. It hurt, but she told them. Everything. Sitting round the new kitchen table, mugs of coffee in front of them, she told them first about Jamie.

In the silence that followed, she could hear the clock in the living-room ticking out the moments of their lives. She could hear a tractor in a distant field. Somewhere sheep bleated. She could hear her father breathing heavily, and giving off a little wheeze at the end of each outward sigh, just like he always had done.

The chair scraped as her mother got up and came round the table to hug her. 'I'm so sorry, love. How terrible. You must feel awful.'

Awful? She supposed she did really.

Or she had done. Now she wasn't sure. She was getting used to it.

'Have you talked to him?'

'Not really, no. He hasn't given me the chance. On the couple of occasions he's rung up, it's just been because he wanted something. No, we haven't talked.'

'Perhaps you should?'

'It's not easy. I don't even know where he is.'

'How long's he been gone?' her father intervened.

'A week or two.'

'And this is the first you've mentioned it to us?'

He sounded angry. Meg didn't know if it was with her or Jamie.

'Leave it, Billy!' her mother said crisply. 'Now's not the time for that.'

'I'd like to get my hands on him,' her father said. 'I would!'

He pushed his chair back and got to his feet.

'There's something else, Dad.'

He looked at her. So did her mother.

'I'm having a baby.'

That news brought another stunned silence. For a moment, at least.

Then her mother clapped her hands, as if with delight. Her father stared at her with astonishment, and then with a broad grin.

'You come on home, Meg, love,' he advised. 'We'll look after you. Never mind that no-good husband of yours. I never did care for him much anyway. A grandson, eh?' he added with a chuckle.

'I don't know that, Dad.'

'Oh, it will be. I've no doubt at all.'

'Well, I have,' Mum intervened.

Suddenly, the atmosphere in the kitchen had changed. Meg had dreaded telling them about the baby, especially when the announcement was fastened on to the news about Jamie, but now she felt glad. She felt happy. Here, at least, was one place where she wasn't alone. It felt so good to be home.

6

Something had woken her. She didn't know what, though, and for a few moments she lay still, listening hard, puzzled. Then she heard it again. The door chain! It was rattling. Someone was trying to get through the front door.

She was petrified. She held her breath and listened, not wanting to hear but unable not to hear. She bit the duvet to stop herself screaming with panic.

She glanced at the clock. Half-past-two. If only she had her mobile with her! But it was downstairs in her bag, which was in the kitchen. She didn't know what to do.

Terrified, she forced herself to get out of bed. She left the light switch alone. Light from the street lamps was enough for her to see her way out of the bedroom. She paused on the landing and gazed down the stairs. The inner door in the hall was closed. Did that mean whoever it was had not got inside yet?

She waited until she heard the chain rattle again. Then, suddenly emboldened, because the noise was coming from the other side of the front door, she made her way downstairs.

She opened the inner-hall door and stared at the big, solid front door. The chain was still in place. And the bolt. But someone was fiddling with the lock. She took a deep breath and switched all the lights on she could reach.

'Go away!' she yelled. 'I'm calling the police.'

The phone was in the hall. She grabbed it and began dialling 999.

'Meg! Is that you?'

She paused, frozen. Then she dropped the phone and her hand flew to her mouth. Jamie!

'Open the door, Meg.'

'What do you want?'

'Come on, Meg! Open the door.'

She grimaced. She recognised the signs. He'd been drinking.

'Go away, Jamie! I mean it. I'm calling the police. I've called them. They're on their way.'

Stand-off. It continued for several minutes. Then there was quiet. She listened. Was he there still?

A car door slammed. The engine started with a roar. The car took off at speed.

She slumped against the wall, exhausted and scared she'd done the wrong thing.

Too late, it occurred to her Jamie was probably in no state to be driving. She should have let him in.

* * *

'So what happened?' Robert asked.

'How do you mean?'

'Well, something has changed in your life. That's obvious.'

She glanced around at the lunch-time crowd, playing for time.

'It's very busy here,' she said, seeing the lines of customers with their trays, the occupied tables everywhere and the harassed staff frantically clearing space for new arrivals.

She knew he was still staring at her, demanding an answer. She sighed and returned his gaze.

'Jamie left me,' she said. 'A few weeks ago.'

'Oh, I'm sorry, Meg.' He grimaced. 'I did wonder . . . Any particular reason?'

She shook her head. 'None I know about. He just . . . just wanted a change, I expect.'

It sounded an unlikely explanation even to her. Not for the first time, she wondered if there was another woman involved.

'No chance of a reconciliation?'

'I don't think so. Not now. There's nothing there any more. I'm over wanting him back, and I'm over blaming myself for him leaving.'

She looked up. Robert said, 'I know what it's like, being on your own.'

'Elizabeth?'

He nodded and added. 'When she died I was devastated.'

He looked it now, too. It wasn't the same thing, though, she thought. Not at all. Worse, probably.

'I had to change something in my life,' he continued. 'So I changed jobs and came here, where people didn't know anything about me. I couldn't bear the thought of any more fuss and sympathy. I just wanted to do my job, and go home to my kids at the end of the day.'

He's just like me, she thought with surprise. I haven't wanted people being sorry for me either.

'Don't ask me why,' he added. 'I can't explain it. I can't explain anything. Not any more.'

'I understand,' she said, touching the back of his hand lightly with her fingers.

He looked her in the eyes and smiled. 'I think you do,' he said softly. 'I really think you do.'

'I've got another problem at the moment,' Robert said. 'I need to go out again tomorrow night, and I was wondering . . . '

'Need a babysitter?'

'Well, *I* don't. But . . . '

'Kirsty and Sean might?'

He nodded and chuckled. 'They liked it when you came that other time. They've never stopped talking about you.'

'I liked them, as well. So what's the problem?'

He paused, thinking something through, and then said, 'If you could manage to help tomorrow night, perhaps we could take you out for lunch at the weekend? Go to the Fish Quay at North Shields.'

'It will be good practice,' she said, 'babysitting.'

He raised an eyebrow.

She gave a wry smile. 'One of the things Jamie left me with was a baby to carry.'

'You're kidding?' he said, staring hard at her.

She shook her head. 'No. I'm pregnant.'

'How do you feel about that?'

'I'm not sure yet. I still haven't got used to the idea.'

He smiled at her.

'What's the problem you were on about?' she asked, glancing at her watch and thinking they couldn't afford to spend much more time over lunch.

He grimaced and said. 'The in-laws.'

'Oh?'

'Don't get me wrong. They're good people, but they're giving me difficulty.'

'What is it?'

He took his time, re-shuffling the salt and pepper pots with the sugar bowl and the milk jug before he replied.

'Well, what it is,' he said, 'is they think the kids would be better off living with them now.'

'Because . . . ?'

'They say a man alone is in no position to look after two young children, and see to their needs, as well as go to work.'

'And how long have you been doing it?'

'Two years.'

'And you haven't been able to prove the point?'

He shook his head. 'They're very nice about it, but they insist they're right.'

'What do you think?'

He pushed his chair back, shrugged and said. 'Sometimes I think they might be right. They're their grandchildren. Maybe I'm not doing everything that's needed.'

'Plenty of women are in your position. Single parents. I'm going to be one, myself, before too long.'

Robert nodded, smiled and pushed his chair back. 'Come on,' he said, his moment of self-doubt apparently over. 'We'd better get back.'

★ ★ ★

Kirsty was adorable, if a little worrying. 'Are you our new Mummy?' she asked.

Meg laughed. 'No, Kirsty, I'm afraid not. But I would like to be your very good friend.'

The little girl seemed satisfied with that. Not too disappointed, anyway. Meg continued helping her get ready for bed.

It was so sad, though, she reflected. Poor little thing. She wouldn't even remember her mother. She just had the idea, the concept of Mummy, in her head. A female version of Daddy, presumably? No. That didn't sound right. She shook her head.

She found Sean watching television. A natural history programme. Elephants were pushing down trees in order to eat the leaves that grew out of reach even of giraffes. He seemed fascinated. Meg quietly settled down to watch the programme with him.

She didn't dare interrupt him with banal questions such as when his bedtime was. He was rapt. A new David Attenborough in the making, she thought with a smile.

'Good?' she asked after the programme finished.

'Yes,' he said solemnly. He hesitated

and then decided to tell her a little about it. 'The mother elephant is the oldest member of the herd, and the most important.'

'Oh?'

'She carries all the herd's secrets and knowledge in her head.'

'Like what?'

She wasn't teasing him, not really, but she did like to hear him thinking. He was such a serious little boy. So solemn!

'Well,' he said judiciously, 'those elephants live in a desert, and the most important thing for them is knowing where to find water.'

'So what do they do?'

'They go to the places where they have always been able to get water. For hundreds of years. Thousands even. Hundreds of thousands.'

'A long time anyway?'

He nodded but wasn't to be deflected. 'Sometimes they have to dig for it, under the sand. They drink all the water in one place. Then they go somewhere else, to another water place. In a few weeks' time they come back to the first one, and the water has built up again.'

He looked at her, still solemn faced.

'What, Sean?'

'The thing is the mother elephant remembers where to go, and takes all the other elephants to the right places. If they couldn't find one of their places, they would have no water and they would die.'

Now she saw what he was driving at, where he was going. But she was unable to deflect him. All she could do was let him see it through to the end.

'She won't forget,' he said quietly, 'but what if she dies? What will happen then?'

'They'll manage, Sean. Somehow they'll manage.'

She reached out and wrapped her arms around him. He came to her and burrowed his face in her neck.

'They might not,' came his muffled whisper.

'They will! The others will remember

her. They will still love her, and remember what she showed them. They will carry on without her, just as she would want them to do.'

'Do you think so?' he asked anxiously.

'Yes! Together, they will manage. After all, there have been elephants in the world for an awfully long time.'

His breathing became regular, with little gasps and snorts occasionally. She risked peering down at him, moving a fold of her jumper slightly to see his closed eyes.

This poor little boy. Such a good little boy. Such a lot on his mind. No wonder he's so solemn.

They were still there, together, when Robert returned. He stood poised in the doorway, a question on his face. She smiled and gently shook her head. He smiled back. There was no problem.

7

Are you doing anything on Saturday?'
Meg asked. Robert raised his eyebrows.
She laughed. 'Don't worry! It's just that
Kirsty said she likes sheep and . . . I
was wondering if you had plans for
Saturday. If not, could I borrow Kirsty?
I'm going to see my parents . . . '

'I'm sure Sean would be pleased.'

'Sean can come as well, if he wants.
You, too, for that matter. I was thinking
of going up to my parents' place. They
live near Alnwick.'

'Lots of sheep there, are there?'

'Any amount. It would give Kirsty
the chance to see the real thing.'

Robert pushed his chair back from
the desk. 'That would be great, Meg.
But are you sure you want to take us?'

'I would enjoy it.'

Saturday came. They travelled north
in Robert's car. All of them. No-one

wanted to miss out on the opportunity to see real, live sheep.

Meg could see her mother was a bit flummoxed. It wasn't surprising.

'Where are your sheep?' Kirsty demanded.

'Sheep? I haven't got any, dear.'

'Oh!'

Disappointment spilled across the kitchen.

'But there's some living in the field at the bottom of the garden,' Mum added.

'But all we have here in the house is a cat. She's got kittens as well. Would you like to see them?'

Kirsty's face lit up and she happily set off outside with her guide.

More happily, her father was soon in conversation with Robert. The two of them went off to see the Morris Minor Shooting Brake her dad was rebuilding — and had been for about fifteen years, to Meg's knowledge.

'That leaves you and me,' Meg pointed out. 'Would you like to see the kittens as well?'

Sean looked around carefully as if to satisfy himself a better option wasn't on offer, and nodded.

Mum had prepared a bountiful lunch, which was enjoyed by all. Robert marvelled over the Morris Minor Shooting Brake. The children played with the kittens and explored the garden. And Kirsty got to see more sheep in the neighbouring field than she had ever imagined existed.

'They're lovely children,' Mum said, as Meg helped her with the washing-up.

Meg agreed

'You said Robert's wife died?'

'Yes. A couple of years ago.'

Mum was quiet for a while after that.

'What?' Meg asked eventually.

'Nothing.'

'Oh, come on!' Meg insisted. 'You've got something on your mind, Mum. I can tell.'

'Well, it's just that you've got enough on your plate, Meg, it seems to me. Here you are, carrying your own baby, Jamie missing, going to work every day

. . . It's too much. You can't wear yourself out with other people's children, as well.'

Meg stopped and stared at her.

'What did you say Robert is?' Mum asked pointedly. 'A friend?'

'I work with him, Mum. And, yes, he is a friend!'

Infuriatingly, her mother inclined her head as if to say — there you are, then!

'Mum, Robert and the children have been the one bright spot in my life lately. I enjoy being with them.'

'But you don't want to do anything that might put Jamie off coming back, do you?'

'Oh, Mum!'

'You don't want your baby to be without a father, do you?'

'What rubbish you talk, Mum! The baby has a father — Jamie. Nothing can take that away. It doesn't matter where Jamie is. He's still . . . Oh, what's the use!'

It was when she opened the curtains the next morning that she saw it for the first time for three months. She recognised it immediately. Her heart began to pound, and she shivered as her face began to burn. Then she stepped back, closed her eyes and tried to work out what it meant.

In the end, she had no alternative. She simply had to know. She ran a brush through her hair quickly, slipped on a pair of sandals and made her way outside to the red BMW.

Jamie looked to be asleep. His head was back against the headrest, his eyes were closed and his mouth was open. Meg stared, and waited a moment while she tried to control her racing heart. Then she rapped on the window.

Jamie's head jerked round. He gazed at her sleepily. Then the lazy smile she knew so well spread slowly across his face. He reached for the handle and opened the door.

'You're a sight for sore eyes, Meg!'

'What are you doing here, Jamie?'

'I came to see you. What do you think?'

'Came to see me?'

Jamie opened the door wide and planted his feet on the pavement.

'What are you doing?' she demanded. Her voice sounded unnaturally shrill even to her.

'Well,' he said with that smile of his that had always opened doors, and her heart, 'I thought I would say hello, and possibly you would give me a peck on the cheek to welcome me home. Then we might go into the house together, maybe have a cup of coffee, and we'd take it from there. How does that sound?'

She was so furious she was blushing. She knew that but she couldn't stop. 'Just like that?' she said.

There were all sorts of things she could have said, and should have said. The thoughts tumbled over each other. But she couldn't get them into any sort of order. The words wouldn't come.

Besides, there were people in the street, people passing by. Some gave them curious looks. A light, cold drizzle began to fall. Meg shivered and turned to head indoors.

She went straight through to the kitchen and grabbed the kettle. While she filled it, she heard the front door slam shut. She closed her eyes for a moment, grimaced and continued.

'I must say it all looks very nice in here,' Jamie said from the doorway. 'So homely and inviting. You've kept things pretty nice, Meg.'

'What did you expect? That the world would fall apart without you?'

'No, not at all. I knew you would cope. You're not like me, Meg. You get ill, or you're depressed, you've got the strength to continue as if nothing's happened. Not like me,' he added with a rueful chuckle, as he lowered himself on to a chair.

It was proving harder than she'd hoped. He'd prepared for this visit, and knew what he wanted out of it. She hadn't — and didn't. It had been thrust upon her without warning, and she didn't know what she wanted. How could she?

'What's that supposed to mean?' she snapped. 'What are you telling me?'

'Nothing, nothing at all!' he assured her with a tired wave. 'That's just how things are. You're strong. I'm not. That's all there is to it. Crisis, and I fall apart. You pick yourself up, and on you go. Not exactly as if nothing's happened, perhaps, but getting on with things.'

She didn't reply. The kettle boiled. She made two mugs of instant coffee and planted them on the table. Then she sat down on the far side.

'What do you want, Jamie?' she demanded. 'You've been gone all this time. Now you turn up at the crack of dawn . . .'

'I didn't want to risk waking you, Meg. So I thought I'd sit in the car for a while and . . .'

'That's not what you thought last time you appeared. It was the middle of the night then. Remember?'

'I must have been drunk,' he said airily. Then he peered closely at her.

'You do look well, Meg! How are you?'

She shrugged that aside and hoped he wouldn't notice she'd put on weight. 'What do you want?' she repeated.

'Want? Me?' He gave her a sad little smile. 'I've come home, Meg, if you'll have me. I've come home.'

She stared at him for a long moment. Then she gave a little yelp, stood up and fled.

8

Having Jamie back was a big fat surprise. That's what Jenny said. Meg agreed with her. 'I didn't think it would ever happen,' Jenny added. 'Not after all this time.'

'He is my husband,' Meg pointed out. 'We are still married.'

'What's that got to do with it?'

'Everything!'

Jenny smiled and laid her hand on top of Meg's. 'Of course it is,' she said. 'You're right. You must be delighted. I'm very pleased for you. Now let's have that coffee. My feet are tired of shopping.'

They headed for their usual coffee spot in the Metrocentre — Santini's.

Delighted? Meg thought, as she made her way to the ladies. To have Jamie back? Was she really?

Yes! She was, she decided firmly. She

was delighted. Just as Jenny said. Happy as could be. She was. Really. But it was going to be a long haul for them to get back on their feet again as a couple. It was going to take time to get over the last three months.

It would for her, at least, she thought ruefully, as she gazed into the mirror. Jamie seemed to think he'd never been away. There had been no betrayal in his mind. His absence had been of no account.

Besides, now there was the baby to think of. He didn't know about that yet. Telling him would be something else that was too soon.

'Are you all right, Meg?'

She spun round. Jenny was in the doorway, looking anxious.

'I think so,' she said.

'Is it the baby?'

Meg nodded. Then she stopped and stared. 'You knew?'

Jenny laughed. 'Of course I did! You can't keep a thing like that secret.'

'You never said anything.'

'Neither did you. So I decided you would tell me when you wanted me to know. You haven't told Jamie yet, by the way, have you?'

'No,' Meg said miserably. 'I'm pleased to have him back. Of course I am. But . . . '

'You'll do right. Take your time.'

Meg hugged her.

There was a delicious smell in the house when she got home. She sniffed appreciatively and smiled. 'You've been baking bread!' she charged as she entered the kitchen.

Jamie turned round from the sink, where he was washing up. He pointed to the wire rack beside the oven.

'Two loaves?' she said. 'You're a genius, Jamie.'

'I know. Have a good time?'

'Yes, thanks. I met Jenny for lunch.'

'How is she?'

'The same as usual.'

He nodded and continued clearing things away. It was extraordinary, she thought, how ordinary everything seemed. Well, almost everything.

'Not working today, Jamie?'

He shook his head. 'The trade's in a bit of a slump. Not so many people are buying new cars at the moment.'

'It must be a pretty big slump, if they're not out buying on a spring Saturday. And even if they're not buying, I'd have thought they would at least be looking.'

'You'd think so, wouldn't you?'

She wandered into the living-room and noted the empty beer cans, and was disappointed. He'd said he'd given up drinking. Still, it was Saturday afternoon, and at least he was home. That made a change.

'Have you been watching something on TV?' she asked, returning to the kitchen.

'Just an old movie. Black and white.'

'What was it?'

'I didn't catch the title.'

'What was it about?'

He shrugged. 'A man and a woman.'

She laughed. 'That must have been good.'

'Well, I had to do something.'

'You could have come shopping.'

'Oh?' He grinned. 'I never thought of that. New shoes? New skirt?'

'New shirt and tie, maybe. That one's a bit crumpled.'

'I've been cooking!'

She laughed and headed upstairs to change. Cooking! she thought. That was new. And so was the crumpled shirt. Jamie had always been immaculate in his appearance.

As she changed, she wondered if she was being too hard on him. He'd been good as gold since he'd returned. Only a week or so, of course, but it was a good start.

He seemed different somehow. She couldn't quite put her finger on it, but there were all sorts of little ways in which he was different. Helping around the house, for one thing. Baking bread even! She almost laughed aloud at that. What would Jenny say?

Then there was the fact that his appearance wasn't what she was used to. He seemed less . . . Well, less immaculate. He'd always ironed his own shirts, because he was better at it than her, and in his job he needed them to be perfect. So he said. Now it didn't look as if he was doing much ironing at all. Not to perfection, anyway. Perhaps it was something to do with his working arrangements changing. He'd said he was in the office more than the showroom now.

'Are we going out tonight?' she called down the stairs.

'I thought we'd stay in, if it's all right with you?' came the reply.

It was perfectly all right with her. But that was something else that was different. Saturday night at home? Jamie? Unthinkable!

★　★　★

'Good weekend, Robert?' Fiona asked.

'Not bad, thanks.'

Meg smiled and kept her head down. She'd got in early in order to write a letter that needed to be sent as a matter of urgency. She wouldn't allow herself to be distracted until it was done.

By ten it was done, and off to the solicitors for perusal before being posted. She could relax. It was a good way to start the week.

'Did you take the kids anywhere nice?' she asked Robert in passing.

'The coast. Whitley Bay.'

She hesitated. 'Meet me for coffee?'

'Sure. Half-an-hour?'

She nodded and pressed on.

The staff room was busy, which was a good thing. Plenty of noisy and chatter. No-one taking particular notice of her, or listening to what she had to say.

She smiled warmly as Robert arrived and sat down.

'It wasn't all plain sailing yesterday,' Robert said as she joined him. 'We could have done with some help.'

'Oh?'

'Kirsty fell down in the sea within the first five minutes. She was soaked.'

'Poor thing! What did you do? Go home?'

'We managed. I wouldn't put it any higher than that. We didn't have a full set of spare clothes in the car, but there was enough to get by with. Anyway, what did you do at the weekend?'

She considered.

'There's something I have to tell you, Robert.'

'Oh?'

'Jamie's come back.'

She watched anxiously as his expression changed, as the thoughts flickered through his head. Then he smiled.

'That's wonderful, Meg! I'm very happy for you.'

She smiled back with relief.

'It's what you wanted, isn't it? What you hoped for?'

'It is. Yes.'

Of course it was. She and Jamie had to patch things up, and move on.

'All couples have difficulties from time to time,' Robert added. 'It's normal. So don't worry about that. The important thing is you're back together again. I hope we'll still see something of you?' Robert said. 'The kids are always asking after you.'

'Of course,' she said. 'There's no reason why not.'

'And Jamie, perhaps?' he added.

'Perhaps.'

Fat chance, she thought. Anything less likely than Jamie agreeing to visit Robert and his children she couldn't imagine. And that, of course, meant she could hardly go herself.

Later, she wondered, sadly, how much Robert would welcome a visit from her now anyway. Things were different now. Everything was different. And better, she reminded herself. Everything was better.

9

The little jewellery box her grand-mother had given her all those years ago was empty. Not a penny in it, never mind the hundred pounds and more she knew had been there a day or two earlier.

Worried, she checked other drawers in the bedroom. Nothing else seemed to be missing, thankfully. And there was no damage. Plenty of small disturbance, but no damage. Not a burglary, then. She blew out with relief. Jamie must have borrowed it. He probably needed some cash urgently. Oh, well. She could put off the shopping trip. It would be a while before Baby arrived.

She made herself some scrambled eggs for tea. Jamie would be a while yet. He worked funny hours these days, and was rarely home in the early evening.

That was the car business, she supposed. As Jamie said, you couldn't close at five o'clock any more. The evening was when so many folk liked to do their shopping these days, whether it was for groceries or for cars.

It seemed to be when people in the car trade did their drinking, as well. Being on the wagon hadn't lasted long. She could smell it on his breath most nights, and now she was pregnant she liked it even less than she always had. It was good to have him back, though, and she wasn't going to complain about anything at all. Certainly not him liking a drink.

They belonged together. Whatever their problems, that couldn't be denied. They would be fine, she told herself once again. Just fine. It wasn't easy at the moment but . . . everyone went through sticky patches. And they were no different to everybody else. Maybe she didn't feel quite the same about Jamie now. How could she? But she had to give it time.

The phone rang. She glanced at the clock. Just after seven. 'Hello, dear. It's only me. I just thought I'd see how you are.'

'Hello, Mum! I thought it would be Jamie. I'm fine, thanks.'

'Where's Jamie?'

'Oh, he's not back from work yet. He works late these days.'

'Earning extra money for the baby, is he?'

She laughed but hoped they could get off that subject quickly.

'Dad and I were so pleased you're both back together again. We're very relieved. It would have been difficult for you on your own. You could have come back to us, of course, but even so . . . '

'I know what you mean, Mum. But it's all behind us now. I don't want to talk or think about it any more.'

'Quite right, too! Silly me. I don't blame you one little bit. Just put it behind you, and get on with your lives. You've got so much to look forward to now.'

Yes, Meg thought uneasily. We have, haven't we?

'Like that nice young man — Robert, was it? — and his children. He's done so well, hasn't he? How awful for him to have lost his wife so young. And the children, their mother. But he's just got on with it, hasn't he? Such lovely children, too.'

It was true. Robert had done well, and was still doing well. He'd put it all behind him, and got on with his life, just like Mum said. Just as she herself was trying to do with Jamie. It wasn't easy, though. A lot easier said than done. She couldn't imagine what Robert had been through.

'That you, Jamie?'

'Most of me anyway.'

She glanced at her watch. Half-nine. It was getting late. She smiled as she heard him wrestling with the door.

'Push it at the bottom!' she called.

It was what you had to do to close it in winter. She got up and went to meet him in the hall.

'You've had a long day,' she pointed out sympathetically.

'And a long evening!' he said, swaying and smiling. 'But here I am, home to the prettiest girl in all the world.'

She smiled and let him hug her, but she evaded his attempted kiss. His breath was making her feel sick.

'Are you hungry?' she asked. 'Do you want something to eat?'

'Eat? No, thanks. Not me. I'm on a diet.'

He staggered towards the lounge, bumping into walls and doors on the way. 'I'll just watch a bit of telly.'

She grimaced. He wasn't supposed to be doing this any more. Maybe nothing had changed after all.

'Have you been driving in this state, Jamie?'

'That old car drives itself, my love. Not a thing to worry about. She knows her own way home. Doesn't really need me.'

She followed him and watched

wearily as he slumped on to the sofa. 'Jamie, I don't want to nag, darling, but it's not good enough. You shouldn't drive if you've been drinking.'

He waved the point aside and struggled with the remote for the TV.

'What if you hit someone?'

'Me? Never had an accident in . . . '

He broke off to concentrate on the buttons.

'Would you like a coffee?' she asked.

'Good idea.'

She felt depressed as she waited for the kettle to heat. In this state, Jamie was a danger to himself and everyone else. And it wasn't unusual. She wondered what, if anything, she could do.

By the time she rejoined him, he'd found some snooker to watch, but without real interest. She wondered if he could actually see it.

Something else came to mind as she sat beside him. 'Jamie, could you let me have that money back you borrowed, please?'

'What money?'

'You know — the . . . '

'I've never borrowed any money.'

'From that little jewellery box on my dressing table.'

'Not me, pet. It must have been somebody else.'

'There is no-one else!'

'Well, it wasn't me,' he insisted.

'Jamie, I was going to go shopping with it for a few things for the . . . '

She stopped. She was annoyed and upset. How stupid he was being! Of course it was him.

Well, she wasn't going to tell him now about the baby, not when he was drunk. She would wait till tomorrow. She could tell him then, and see if she could get more sense out of him then about the money as well. He probably didn't know what he was saying at the moment.

10

I haven't got long for lunch today,'
Jenny said as she dumped her bag on
the table. 'But before I forget, can you
and Jamie come round on Friday night?
We haven't seen you for ages.'

Meg forked a piece of tomato in her
salad, and tried to avoid the mayon-
naise that went with it.

'I'd better say no, Jenny. Thanks all
the same.'

'Not well? Tired?'

'No, it's not that. I'm fine. It's Jamie.
His hours are so unpredictable these
days. He usually works late in the
evening, as well.'

'Why's that?'

'Something to do with re-organisation.
His job seems to have changed.'

Jenny nodded and concentrated on
her soup for a moment. 'Microwaves!'
she said with disgust, pushing the bowl

aside. 'This is far too hot.'

'Better too hot than too cold,' Meg pointed out with a mischievous grin.

'You sound like my mother.'

'Anyway,' Meg said, 'apart from being too busy, how are things with you?'

'Fine, thanks. But Mike's on about changing his car again. So I'm getting a bit bored with hearing about fuel consumption and 0-60 performance statistics.'

Meg laughed. 'It doesn't seem long since he last changed his car.'

'It isn't. But he wants an estate. So he can put the dogs in the back, and not worry about hairs all over the seats and sticking to his posh suits.'

'He'll need a big estate for those dogs.'

Jenny nodded. 'If it was down to me, I'd have Yorkies. But German Shepherds seem to be a virility statement.'

Jenny finished her soup and glanced at her watch. 'Time for coffee?' Meg asked.

'Just. You sit there. I'll get them.'

Meg was glad to sit and relax for a moment, content to be waited on. She seemed to get so tired these days. Because of the baby, presumably.

'Jamie's new job,' Jenny said when she returned. 'Where is it?'

'Oh, he's still at Sutton's. The same place. He's not moved.'

Jenny placed the cups on the table and found somewhere to deposit the tray. Then she sat down. 'I don't want to worry you, Meg,' she said slowly, 'but are you sure?'

'About what?'

'His job.'

'Of course I am! What a funny thing to say. Why do you ask?'

Jenny shrugged and drew breath. 'Well, it's just that he wasn't there when Mike called in to see him.'

'Oh?'

'Mike thought he'd look in on him when he was going round the showrooms. Get some advice. But he wasn't there.'

'He'll have been busy. Out with a customer, I expect.'

Jenny shook her head. 'No. I don't think so. He's not there at all now. He doesn't work there any more. That's what they said.'

Meg felt herself colouring. 'What on earth do you mean?' she demanded.

Jenny grimaced. 'That's what they said. What they told Mike. He hasn't been there for two or three months, apparently.'

Meg stared hard at her, willing her to be joking.

Jenny shrugged. 'The funny hours you were on about? I think you should ask him what's going on. I would,' she added unnecessarily.

'Damn you!' Meg said, the blood rushing to her brain, the heat to her face.

She jumped up. 'Keep out of our affairs, Jenny! It's nothing to do with you.'

'Meg! I . . . '

Meg flung a five-pound note on the

table and stalked off.

She was so upset she didn't return to work. She kept going, all the way back home.

She used her mobile to call the office from the bus. Robert answered. Probably he was the only one not out for lunch.

'I'm not coming back this afternoon, Robert. Tell them, will you, please?'

'Are you OK?'

He sounded worried.

'No, I'm not feeling well. So I thought I'd better get away home. I'll be all right, but it's best for me to go and lie down.'

'Well, take care! Do you hear?' After a moment's pause, he added, 'And let me know if there's anything I can do.'

She thanked him and ended the call. Dear Robert! She thought with a wistful smile. What a lovely man. Even that short conversation had calmed her down and made her feel better. She would ring Jenny later and apologise. Jenny had meant well. She knew that.

It was peaceful in her street. No traffic. Hardly any parked cars. Children all at school or toddlers' groups. Parents at work. Or watching TV. Spring now, she realised with surprise. The handful of bare-boned trees along the pavement were getting used to the idea, and one or two were even sprouting tentative leaves. Season of hope.

Her step faltered as she neared their house. Music was pounding through the open window. Some terrible loud rock music. Heavy metal. Jamie's music. She stood for a moment. Then she grimaced and pressed on with determination. She needed to get to the bottom of this.

The front door was ajar. She walked through into the lounge and stopped, astonished, at the sight of Jamie laid out on the sofa, conducting the music with a beer can in hand.

Anger surged through her. She crossed the room and switched everything off.

Jamie sat up, looking even more surprised than she felt.

'Well?' she said, glaring at him. 'What's going on?'

'Hi, Meg! Going on? Nothing. Just taking it easy. Chilling. That's all.'

He beamed at her. His speech wasn't slurred, but she could tell he'd had a few drinks. He always lapsed into this good-humoured, innocent little boy mode when he'd been drinking. She wasn't put off.

'Why aren't you at work, Jamie?'

Go on! she urged silently. Tell me something I can believe, something I can live with. For once, don't lie to me. Please, Jamie!

'Flexible working, Meg. You should know all about that, working for the council. No such thing as nine-to-five any more.'

'Is that the truth, Jamie?'

He looked at her, surprise in his eyes. He gave his nervous little laugh.

'You're not going to tell me, are you?' she said quietly, anger giving way to despair.

'Tell you what?' he said sullenly, the jovial bluster gone now.

'You don't work at Sutton's any more, do you?' she said, seeing the truth for herself at last. 'Jenny was right. You don't work anywhere, in fact.'

He was all set to deny it, to laugh it off. But something in her face, or her voice, changed his mind. He shook his head and slumped back on to the sofa.

To her dismay, he began to weep.

'Jamie!' she said. 'Oh, Jamie!'

11

Knowing didn't make it any easier. In fact, it made things worse. Now she could no longer hide from the truth, and it hurt. They were in trouble.

Jamie didn't seem to see it like that, though. If anything, he was happier now the truth was out and he no longer had to pretend.

'I'll soon have another job,' he told her. 'Sutton's isn't the only car dealer on the planet!'

'Have you been looking, Jamie? Seriously?'

'Of course I have! I've got feelers out all over the place. As a matter of fact, I've had approaches made to me. Head hunters, you know. I'm not going to rush into anything. I'll wait till the right deal comes along, the right deal for me, that is.'

Her spirits plummeted when she

heard him talking like that. Increasingly, as the weeks rolled by, it sounded like bluster. Typical Jamie, she realised. The gift of the gab that had launched him on his salesman's career, a career that seemed to have fizzled out now, thanks to his drinking. She couldn't help comparing it with the sensible, modest talk she heard from Robert. Jamie didn't even sound funny any more.

The worst of it, though, was the drinking. It grew steadily worse, now he had no need to hide his circumstances from her eyes. Morning and afternoon. Evenings, as well. Not all the time, of course, but a good part of every day.

Money disappeared, too. What she brought into the house was soon spent. The overdraft on her account grew. But that was only part of it. For a long time — ever since she was a little girl, in fact — she had been in the way of setting small accounts of money, actual cash, aside in little hiding places. Now those hiding places were empty.

In desperation, she decided finally to tell him about their baby. That would make a difference. Surely it would? It had to.

'I've got some news for you, Jamie,' she said carefully as they sat around the breakfast table.

'Oh?'

'We're going to have a baby.'

He looked up from the guide to the day's racing he was studying, stared for a moment and then broke into raucous laughter. 'You never told me!' he charged. 'When?'

'The end of August.'

He got up and hugged her, laughing with delight. She knew he meant it. He really was pleased. She smiled and hugged him back, pressing her face into him. The moment she had been dreading turning out to be perfect. Perhaps they would turn the corner at last.

She closed her eyes and held on to him.

'Happy?' she asked.

'What do you think? Of course I am. Why didn't you tell me earlier? Oh, I know! Of course. I've been really stupid, haven't I?'

She nodded, still smiling. He laughed again. The old Jamie! He'd reappeared.

'Things have to change, though, Jamie. We can't go on like we have been.'

'I know, I know! I'll get a job. Soon. I promise.'

'It's not just that, though, is it? I mean, the money's important. Of course it is. But you can't carry on drinking like you have been. That's the main problem.'

'You're right. Of course you are. I'll stop. I don't need it. It's just been that it's a long day . . . Oh, you know!'

'Maybe you should get help, Jamie. It would be easier. Get counselling. Go to one of these therapy groups?'

He broke away, still laughing. 'Can you see me, Meg? Can you? In a room full of people. We're all sitting there, and one after another we have to say how much we hate the drink, how we're going to stop right now. Is that what you see?'

'No, of course not,' she said, uncomfortable with the picture he was painting. 'But why not see the doctor? See what he says. You have a problem, Jamie. We have a problem. We need help.'

'I'll cut down. I promise. It's only fair.'

She was glad she'd told him about the baby at last. Perhaps that would do it. Perhaps everything would be different now.

★ ★ ★

'Has he been applying for jobs?' Jenny asked.

'Yes. Of course, he has. Well, I think he has. He says he has.'

She frowned. She knew what Jenny was thinking. They had patched things up between them. Meg was glad.

She had no better friend than Jenny.

'You can't go on like this,' Jenny said gently. 'It's wearing you out. He's not worth it.'

Meg kept quiet. She wished she hadn't said anything now.

'How long has he been gone this time?'

'Five days.'

'What does he say when he comes back?'

'It's as if nothing ever happened. He just seems to think everything's wonderful.'

'That's what I mean,' Jenny said. 'You can't go on like this. What are you doing for money?' she asked. 'Are you managing all right?'

Straight to the point! Meg couldn't help smiling.

'Of course we are. There's still my salary.'

'And his redundancy money? There must have been a fair bit of that.'

'Yes,' Meg said thoughtfully. 'There must have been, mustn't there?'

They stared at one another for a long moment.

'And how long was he away that first time?' Jenny asked with a heavy sigh.

'A couple of months. Three.'

'And he went abroad?'

'He got me to send him his passport. I don't know what he did with it.'

Jenny snorted and shook her head. 'Where's all his drinking money coming from?' she asked, laying her hand on Meg's wrist.

'I don't know,' Meg said miserably.

But she knew where some of it was coming from. Or where it had been coming from, until all her little caches were gone.

Jenny sat up straight. 'Don't say it!' Meg warned sharply. 'He's my husband, and we have a happy marriage. We've put our problems behind us. And we're going to be a very happy family.'

'Of course you are,' Jenny said.

Meg stared off into space. She didn't think either one of them truly believed that.

The house was dark and empty, and cold. Meg shivered and hurried to put the heating back on. No sign of Jamie. Perhaps he was out job hunting? She gave a weary smile. Perhaps he wasn't. But she mustn't be critical. He was doing his best.

She heated up some soup and settled down with it in front of the television to watch the early evening news. When the programme finished she switched the television off and sat for a while, just thinking. It wasn't good for her. Thinking. She knew that. It could make her panic. What on earth were they to do? How were they to manage?

The reality was that Jamie still didn't have a job. He didn't seem much concerned either. His days were full enough. He met friends in the pub at lunch-time, and met them again later in the day. He talked the talk about job hunting — nobody better — but she could see precious few signs he was actually doing anything about it.

As for herself, she was running on empty now. She was physically and mentally exhausted. Her thoughts, and what energy she had left, had to be focussed on the life growing within her. That was more than enough. She'd been doing her best, but she couldn't sort out Jamie's problems as well. He was supposed to be supporting her!

She stirred. She couldn't sit here like this all night again, wallowing in self-pity. She needed someone to talk to. And she needed to get out of the house for a while. She needed distraction.

It was no good thinking of Jenny either. She'd heard enough advice from Jenny, whose opinion was that she should kick Jamie out. But it wasn't that easy. It was all right for Jenny to say these things. But she didn't have the problem. Jamie wasn't her husband.

She picked up the phone and pressed the buttons. No answer. She tried again. The same thing. For a long time there was no answer. Sadly, she put the phone down and wandered back into the kitchen. There were pots to wash.

As the hot water streamed into the

bowl she heard the phone ring. Jamie, probably. Wanting to explain why he'd be home late again. Some story about a job possibility, and needed to see a man in a pub about it. Or a club. A restaurant even. Jamie's stories were endlessly inventive.

She reached for a towel and dried her hands as she walked back to the phone.

'Hi, Meg! Did you just call me?'

She closed her eyes for a moment and then smiled with pleasure. 'Yes, Robert. I did.'

'Sorry I didn't get to the phone in time. Bath time, I'm afraid. You know how it is.'

'Not yet, I don't!'

'Soon, then. You will soon. How are you anyway? I don't seem to have had time to talk to you lately.'

Not since the news of Jamie's return, she thought. She knew what he was doing. He was keeping well. He knew she had enough to do and think about, without helping him look after his kids.

'I'm fine, Robert, thank you. Looking

forward to the day. What about Kirsty and Sean?'

'The same. Full of trouble.'

'Get away! You're terrible. They're wonderful children.'

'Only joking. They're OK. They keep asking after you, by the way. We'll have to get together again soon. They still talk all the time about that day up in Northumberland.'

She chuckled. Her heart wasn't in it, but she did.

'How's Jamie?'

'Oh, he's busy as ever. Changing his job and . . . '

'I'm happy for you, Meg. I really am. It's so good the two of you have sorted things out.'

'Thanks, Robert. You've been a good friend.'

'Hear that? It sounds like the Atlantic has reached the bathroom. I'd better go before the bath floats out to sea. Nice to hear you, Meg.'

Afterwards, after she had put the phone down, she realised how much she had missed Robert lately. The children, too, of course, but she had missed Robert himself. He was such fun, and so lively. Such a good person to be with. Such a good person.

Stop! She told herself. That's enough. Jamie was her husband. She needed to concentrate on him, if their life was to be better. Besides, to Robert, she was just an occasional babysitter. Child minder, rather. Colleague. And friend. She shouldn't let herself get carried away, nice man or not.

It was after midnight when she heard Jamie stumble into the house. She was in bed by then, feeling depressed and weary. At least he was home safe, she thought duly. Then she lay still and listened to him blundering around the kitchen, rattling pans, turning the tap on. Hungry, probably.

She stirred herself and got out of bed. She put on her dressing gown and headed down the stairs.

'Jamie! What are you doing, love?' By the time she reached the kitchen, he was singing happily and clattering the frying pan.

'Bacon and eggs!' he announced gleefully. 'I'm cooking. Want some?'

'There isn't any bacon, I'm afraid.'

'Eggs, then. I'll fry some eggs.'

'Jamie, do you know what time it is?'

'Not really, no.'

'It's gone midnight, Jamie. And I have go to work in the morning.'

'Get yourself off to bed, then. I can manage.'

She doubted that. 'Where have you been, Jamie?'

'Checking up on me, are you?'

Suddenly his tone had changed. He spun round, eyes flashing. 'Not for the first time either. I'm sick of it!'

'I'm expecting a baby, Jamie — our baby! And you leave me alone, like this? I'm tired, worn out, and I need your help and support.'

'And you have it! Just don't interfere. Don't tell me what I can and can't do.'

'We can't afford for you to be out every night like this, Jamie. Round the pubs, drinking. There's only my salary now to pay for everything.'

'Money, money, money!' he sneered. 'That's all you think about.'

'It's not good for you either,' she continued. 'You know it isn't. You promised, Jamie!'

He swore at her and suddenly picked the pan up and flung it across the kitchen. It hit the wall. Fat dripped.

'I'm going where I'm more welcome!' he shouted. 'Where someone doesn't pick on me all the time.'

He barged past her and thundered through the hall. She heard the front door slam. Moments later, his BMW roared into life. She listened as it raced down the street and screeched round a corner. Then she collapsed on to a hard wooden chair, sobbing. What on earth was she to do?

12

Meg, I hate to ask, but could you possibly stay with Kirsty for an hour after work?'

'What is it, Robert?'

He grimaced and ran a hand through his hair. 'Another little crisis! The school's just rung. Sean's had an accident. Nothing serious. But he had to have stitches in his head, and they want me to collect him from the hospital. So I need someone to look after Kirsty for me.'

'Of course. I'd be glad to help.'

She rang home but there was no answer, which wasn't surprising. She never knew where Jamie was these days. His good intentions hadn't lasted long.

'I haven't seen much of you lately,' Robert said as they walked out to his car. 'How have you been?'

'Pretty good, thanks. The bump's

getting bigger, though,' she added, patting her stomach.

'Call that a bump? That's nothing!'

'Well, it feels like a mountain to me. Anyway, how have you been?'

'Struggling.' He grinned. 'They run me ragged, the pair of them.'

'I don't believe it. You're an old softy!'

'Old, yes,' he said, opening the passenger door and helping her into the car. 'And as soft as a lump of concrete.'

Meg laughed. Already she felt better. Five minutes with Robert, and . . . How was that possible?

'What's Sean been up to?' she asked as they set off.

'Just playing football, I think. That's what they said anyway. Banged his head on something harder than him.'

First, they collected Kirsty from the childminder. She was thrilled. 'Meg! I didn't know you were coming for me.'

Meg laughed and hugged her. Kirsty was so excited it was infectious. Her eyes shone. Her face was all smiles.

Golden curls tumbled across her face. Jam round her mouth soon transferred to Meg's face.

'I'm just coming for a little while,' Meg said. 'Daddy's going to collect Sean.'

Robert dropped them off at the house. 'I'll be as quick as I can,' he assured Meg.

'Don't worry about that. Just go and see to Sean. Don't worry about us.'

He gave her a smile that warmed her heart. She sighed and shook her head wistfully as she listened to him drive away. How was it that he made her feel so happy?

Sean wasn't too good. He was tired and subdued. He managed a smile for Meg, and a quiet hello, but not much more. He didn't even respond to Kirsty's shrill enquiries about his bandaged head. Robert put him to bed.

'He'll be all right?' Meg asked anxiously.

'I think so. He's just tired and

over-wrought. Maybe a bit concussed, as well, they said at the hospital. It's been a long day for him, poor lad.'

'For you, too,' she pointed out.

He yawned and glanced at his watch. 'I'm sorry, Meg. It's late. I've been longer than I thought.'

'Doesn't matter.'

'Jamie will be worried to death. Did you call him?'

She shook her head. 'No,' she said. 'But I don't think he'll be worried at all.'

Robert stared at her, and after a moment said, 'What's wrong, Meg?'

'The same thing,' she said with a weary shrug. 'Nothing's changed.'

'He's not gone off again, has he?'

She nodded. 'He's in and out. Here for a while. Then gone again. Drinking more heavily than ever. Lost his job because of it.'

She shrugged and added, 'I haven't see him at all the last three days.'

'What on earth's wrong with him?' Robert demanded angrily.

She shook her head.

'Does he know about the baby?'

She nodded.

'And it hasn't made any difference?'

'For a day or two it did. While the idea was a novelty.'

Robert slammed his hand down on the table. She jerked her head back with shock 'Sorry, Meg. It's just . . . '

He gave up, shaking his head, perplexed. She knew how he felt. 'I'm glad I've told you,' she said. 'I can't bear having to lie and pretend to everyone all the time. My life should be wonderful. Everyone thinks it is. But it's not.'

'It will be,' he said fiercely. 'Jamie's got to see sense.'

She stayed at Robert's a while, and had a cup of coffee with him. There was nothing for her to rush back home for. Even if Jamie had turned up again, she knew what he'd be like. Uninterested in her, or in much else.

'I'm starving,' Robert announced. 'How about some ham and eggs?'

She pulled a face. 'You go ahead,' she told him.

'You must be hungry?'

'I'm more a pasta person.'

'Macaroni cheese?'

She smiled. Why not? She was a bit peckish.

Later, as they ate, Robert said, 'Do you know, I can't remember the last time I ate a meal with another adult. Probably at your mother's, that day. It's good,' he added with a shy smile.

'I know how you feel.'

'Oh, I'm sorry! I didn't think . . . '

She waved the apology aside.

'You haven't got used to being on your own, have you?' she asked.

He shrugged. 'I wouldn't say that, exactly. I'm used to it, all right, but I can't say I like it.'

'You must have had a good marriage?' she suggested.

'I suppose we did. We didn't think of it in that way, though. I didn't anyway. It was just . . . well, ordinary. We were happy enough. Enjoyed life. Loved each other. There were ups and downs, of course, but we'd known each other since we'd started school. We were used to each other. No problems, apart from the usual ones — not enough money, too small a house, too old a car, too near in-laws . . . '

He broke off when she laughed. Then he grinned and added. 'That sort of thing. Yes. It was a good marriage. We were happy. But all that came to an end, and there was nothing I could do about it. You and Jamie, though. You've still got a chance.'

Meg wondered if that was still true. Was Robert right? Or was Jenny? Perhaps their happy time was over, too.

How much easier it would be if Jamie was more like Robert!

13

She surfaced slowly. The sea was deep at that point. Dark blue, fading into black. Beautiful. Absorbing. Mysterious shapes moving all around her. But the alarm bell had startled her. A good thing, too. She was running out of air. Reluctantly, she headed for the surface.

She lay still, gazing at the snowflake patterns on the ceiling made by the street lights shining through the curtains. She smoothed her face with her hands, wiping away the beads of moisture on her forehead. Exciting though it had been, she was relieved to be out of that dream.

Then she frowned as the alarm bell rang again. Now, though, she knew it was the front-doorbell. She got out of bed, moved the curtain slightly aside and peered out into the street. As usual at night, both sides were lined with parked cars. One car, a couple of houses away, had lights on and the engine was running. She couldn't see any other signs of life.

The doorbell rang again, making her heart flutter. She glanced at the clock on the bedside table. It was just after three.

She wasn't sure what to do. She called Jamie's name, but she knew he wasn't there. She went out on to the landing and called again. Still no answer. He wasn't in the house. He hadn't been home for a day or two. She would have to go to the door herself. Whoever was there wasn't going to give up.

She put on a couple of lights and began to make her way downstairs. Halfway there the thought came to her that it might be an emergency with her parents. Something had happened! Something terrible.

She opened the inner door to the hall.

'Who is it?' she called.

'Police officers, madam!' a woman's voice replied. 'We need to speak to you.'

She put the outside light on. Through the narrow glass pane beside the door, she saw two figures in uniform. A man and a woman. The woman stepped up close, announced herself and held up a badge in a folder.

'What's wrong?' Meg asked, opening the door as far as the safety chain would allow. 'What's happened?'

'Mary Anne Armstrong?'

Meg hesitated and then nodded.

'I'm sorry, Mary. We need to speak to you. May we come inside?'

'It's very late,' Meg said, confused, worried.

'I know, dear. But it really is urgent. Please?'

She unlatched the chain, opened the door, turned and led the way into the lounge. She switched on the light. Nobody sat down. The three of them stood around awkwardly. They were too big for that small room. Too close together.

'Mary . . . ' The police woman began.

'Meg.'

'Excuse me?'

'I'm known as Meg, not Mary. Always have been.'

The woman nodded. 'Meg, then. I'm sorry to have to tell you, Meg, but we have bad news. It might be better if you sat down.'

Meg stood quite still, ignoring the suggestion. 'What is it?' she demanded. 'Is it Dad? My mother?'

The woman shook her head. 'Your husband, I'm afraid.'

Meg gasped. Her hand flew to her mouth. She hadn't thought of that possibility. 'Jamie?'

The woman nodded. 'I'm afraid he's dead, Meg. He was killed in a car crash tonight. Last night, I mean. On the A1, in Durham. I'm very sorry, dear.'

Jamie? Dead?

Panic overtook her. She began to gabble questions even as the tears began to flow. Her body lurched with fear and shock. She felt faint. Dizzy.

The man caught hold of her and lowered her into a chair. She bounced straight back up and began to cannon between furniture and walls. No, no, no! It couldn't be true.

The craziness passed. The panic subsided, giving way to piercing hurt. And anger. Rage. Then that, too, passed and she was just numb. The policewoman sat her down on the sofa and spoke to her slowly, calmly. Saying things that for a moment she couldn't hear, never mind understand. Nothing made sense. Her baby! What would she do? Without Jamie!

'All we know, Meg, is that his car left the road not far from Durham City. It was travelling north. It seems to have spun at an intersection and cut across on to the other side of the road. A lorry travelling south hit it head-on.'

Meg stared at her blankly, wanting more, wanting her to keep talking and to tell her it wasn't true, that Jamie would be coming home.

'Your husband was killed instantly.

I'm sorry,' the woman added.

Meg's gaze shifted to the floor, as if she might see more sense there.

'Do you know where he'd been?' the woman asked.

Meg shook her head. How could she know that? 'Had he been drinking?' she asked.

The woman hesitated. Then she gave a little nod. 'Probably,' she admitted. 'We believe he had.'

Meg bowed her head. Oh, Jamie! she thought with despair. My poor, dear Jamie. His face filled her eyes, his voice her head. But it was the Jamie from long ago she saw, from when they were first together, first married. The hurt and disappointments from recent times were forgotten.

The police officers brought Jenny over to be with her. They couldn't stay but they would return, they said. Meanwhile, here was her friend.

Meg had never been so glad to see Jenny. She clung to her, sobbing. Jenny let her, and said nothing. There was nothing worth saying.

It was a long night. Meg didn't return to bed. She couldn't think of lying down. She just sat, frozen. Jenny made cups of tea and busied herself around the house, doing goodness knows what. Later, Meg heard her talking to her mother on the phone. Later still, her mother arrived. And Dad.

Then, for a while, she wasn't aware of anything that was happening. All she could think of was Jamie. And their baby. What would happen to them all now?

14

Meg soon became used to life at Bracken Cottage again. At times, it was as if she had never been away. Everything was so familiar, and so peaceful. Almost too much so. At times she missed the roar of traffic, the screech of tyres as someone took the corner too fast at the end of the street. The street lights, too, that created such patterns on the bedroom ceiling.

At times she even missed Jamie, but not much, if she was honest. Not as much as she would have thought, once she'd got over the shock. It seemed to her now that Jamie had been gone from her long before that terrible night when he died. So what she missed were their first years together. There had been little to delight her in more recent times. Besides, she had more urgent demands on her now.

She stirred herself, climbed out of bed and turned sideways to admire her profile in the mirror. Not long to go now. Some days it was as if the baby was about to tear himself out into the new world, without help from anyone. She smiled. She knew it was a boy. She just knew it.

'How are you this morning, dear?'

She turned, still smiling. 'Fine thanks, Mum. I'll be even better in a week or two's time!'

'Of course you will.'

Mum smiled back and added, 'I remember how fed up I used to get carrying you. Impatient too, for it to be over. But you were worth it.'

'Thanks, Mum! And so will this little fellow be.'

'Girl, you mean.'

Meg shook her head decisively. 'He's a boy.'

'Do you know from the scan?'

'No, I just know.'

Mum laughed. 'Dad will be pleased. Someone to help dig the garden and build sheds.'

She was right — James! He was born right on time in the maternity hospital in Alnwick. She named him after his father, feeling that was the right thing to do. He was Jamie's continuing stake in the world.

At 8 lb 4 oz James was a big boy from the start, and ready to delight everyone he saw.

'Look at those eyes!' Mum said. 'He's wide awake already, after just a few hours.'

'Nearly ready to give me a hand in the garden,' Dad said with satisfaction, and with a wink at Meg.

She laughed. She was unbelievably happy. Holding James gave her an extraordinary feeling, better than anything she had ever experienced.

Mum and Dad were so good with him, too. That was lovely. James seemed to know instinctively that he was part of a family that would cherish him.

It would have been so much better, of course, if Jamie had been here as well to hold his son, but that hadn't been meant to be. Even if he'd been alive, she doubted if he would have been here anyway. Not for long. The old Jamie would, of course. The young Jamie, rather. The Jamie she had loved more than anything or anybody in the world, and who had loved her back just as much. And that was the Jamie she would remember and tell James about as he grew up.

The girls in the office had kept in touch over the months since Meg had left work. Carol and Fiona came to see her that first evening in hospital. They were suitably impressed.

'He's perfect,' Carol said with longing. 'Nice blond hair, blue eyes, tall . . . He's got everything.'

'Do you know how long you'll be here in hospital?' Fiona asked.

'Not long, apparently. I might be leaving tomorrow. That's what the nurses say anyway.'

'Oh? Robert will be disappointed.'

Meg blinked. 'Robert?'

'It's just that he wanted us to ask you

if he could visit. His children want to see the baby, apparently.'

'Of course they can visit!'

'But if you're not here . . . ?'

'He can come to Mum's. I'll be staying there, and he knows where it is.'

'Does he?' Carol said, looking interested.

'He's been before.'

'Has he now?' Carol and Fiona said in unison, with sideways glances and giggles at one another.

'Honestly, you two!'

Later that evening, Jenny and Mike arrived. 'How wonderful!' Jenny cried, seeing baby James for the first time. 'I've always wanted one of them.'

'Congratulations, love!' Mike said, stooping to kiss Meg. 'Haven't you done well?'

'Thank you, Mike. You're too kind. All I did was double in size and carry a large weight around for the best part of nine months.'

Mike patted his ample stomach and said, 'I know how it feels.'

'Take no notice of him,' Jenny advised. 'He has no idea what we women have to put up with.'

Meg laughed. It was good to have company.

Then more arrived. 'Kirsty? Is it really you?' Meg cried with delight. 'What are you doing here?'

'Come to see you, of course!'

It was indeed Kirsty. She climbed up on to the bed and gave Meg a kiss. Then she spotted James and rushed to peer into his cot.

'Kirsty?' Jenny murmured.

'Robert's little girl. Robert from the office. Oh, here they are! Sean and Robert.'

Suddenly there was a swarm of people around her, and a terrible shortage of chairs. Robert kissed her cheek. 'It's good to see you, Meg. You're looking well, too. And this is . . . ?' he added, peering at the new arrival.

'James!' Kirsty cried.

Back at Bracken Cottage, fatigue

caught up with Meg. Fatigue and James's needs. It was lovely to have him to herself, but it was so tiring. She had never been so tired. She was physically and mentally exhausted, drained.

'But so happy!' she told Mum, who smiled and left her to feed James.

Jenny came on her own to visit after a couple of days. 'How's it going?' she wanted to know.

Meg rolled her eyes and smiled. 'It's topsy-turvy, but I'm getting used to it.'

'You're both looking very well, anyway. And I swear James is bigger already.'

'He should be. What an appetite!'

They chatted for a minute or two. Then Jenny said, 'I hope your other visitors got home all right the other night. Have you heard from them?'

'Robert, you mean? No, I haven't. Why, was there a problem?'

'Something not right with his car, apparently. It was probably all right, though. What a dishy man, by the way. You've never mentioned him, have you?'

Meg shrugged awkwardly. 'I can't remember. He's just someone I work with. That's all.'

Meg settled into life with Baby James very easily. She had plenty to do, and plenty to think about. Somewhere ahead a return to work beckoned, but she was happy to let that come towards her slowly. Jenny kept her in touch with events in town, such as they were, and her frequent visits to Bracken Cottage were very welcome. Not everything she said was, though.

'Have you heard from Robert?' Jenny asked on one of those occasions.

'No. Should I have?'

'Well, he seemed very fond of you.'

'Jenny! He's a friend, and a colleague. That's all.'

'Anything you say.'

Meg didn't know whether to be amused or exasperated.

'Anyway,' Jenny added, 'What are you planning on doing? Staying here at Great Newton a bit longer? I should, if I were you.'

'I don't know. I've been here six months already.'

'So what? It's nice here. And it must help, having ready-made babysitters.'

'That's true. But I'm thinking of going back to Gosforth soon. I'll have to start preparing for my return to work.'

'Do you want me to do anything in the house?'

'No, it's all right, thanks. Dad's been going down every week, to keep an eye on things. He says the house is fine.'

'Have you been back yourself?'

Meg shook her heard and then paused uncertainly. 'I'll have to one day, though. I suppose. Or sell it. I'm not sure how easy it will be to move back in there.'

'Well, there's no hurry. Take your time. The house can wait. So can the job, for that matter. Your maternity leave has a bit to go yet, doesn't it?'

Meg nodded.

'Anyway,' Jenny added, with a glance at her watch, 'lovely though it is here, and wonderful as it's been to see you and James again, I must be off. His lordship will be awaiting my return anxiously.'

After Jenny had left, Meg's thoughts turned to Robert, who would probably meet Jenny's requirements for a man. She wondered if he really was fond of her. It would be nice, she decided with a smile, however unlikely. She would quite like him to be fond of her.

Oh, she did miss Robert! And Kirsty and Sean. She missed them all. And it was such a long time since she'd seen them. She hoped they were well, and happy. And she wondered if they missed her just a little bit, as well.

A cry from James diverted her, and stopped the tears that were threatening to fall. She got up to see him,.

'But I've got you now, haven't I?' she told him as he gurgled happily away at her. 'And you mean more to me than anything in the whole wide world.'

Baby James looked as if he understood every word, and as if he believed her implicitly. All the same, she thought, once she was back in Gosforth she would contact Robert. She would ring him just to see how they all were.

She returned to her own house soon afterwards. She had been putting it off but she knew she had to do it sometime. Apart from anything else, she needed to sort out a childminder for James. Maternity leave wasn't going to last forever, unfortunately, and she needed time to find someone reliable to look after James when the day came.

Jenny soon rediscovered the route to her front door, and they developed a new routine of going to the supermarket together. It made grocery shopping less of a chore. Besides, Jenny had a car of her own with, surprisingly, a child seat already fitted.

'I thought I would need it one day,' Jenny said wistfully.

'You will!' Meg assured her, knowing how much she longed for a baby. 'Don't worry so much.'

'You're right. Meanwhile, it's handy

anyway. Come on, Baby James!'

Meg smiled. Dear Jenny! She was never down for more than a minute at a time.

'By the way,' Jenny added, 'you'll never guess who was asking after you the other day.'

'I don't suppose I will, no. You'd better tell me.'

'Robert. You know? The man you work with?'

'I know who Robert is, Jenny.'

'Of course you do. Well, anyway, I bumped into him in Fenwicks. We had a nice chat. He was asking after you.'

'Oh?'

'I told him you were back in your house now. I also told him he should give you a call.'

Meg felt her face flush. To hide her confusion, she leaned down to rearrange James's covers. 'I'm not interested, Jenny,' she said over her shoulder. 'He's a friend, that's all. Besides, he's faithful to the memory of his wife. He's a one-woman man. You ought to be able to see that.'

Jenny shrugged. 'Circumstances change,' she said mysteriously.

'This place!' she said then, turning round to look along the collections of vegetables that stretched away into the distance. 'It's so big, so huge, it takes me twice as long to do my shopping.'

'You need roller blades, like some of the staff have,' Meg said, pointing to a young shelf stacker ghosting like the wind past the cereal section, heading rapidly for crisps and soft drinks.

'Besides,' Jenny added, 'I get lost. I don't know where anything is any more. It's all very well stocking everything under the sun but if you can't find the simplest thing, what's the use?'

Meg chuckled. They finished loading their trolleys and moved on to the checkout, and out to the car park, for Jenny to run them home.

Before they parted, Jenny said, 'You can tell me to mind my own business if you like, Meg, but I really do think you should give Robert a call. Let him know you're back in town. He'll be pleased.'

She meant to take Jenny's advice. She really did. But she didn't. Moving back into her house and looking after James and herself was more than enough to do and think about. She would, though, she promised herself. She would call Robert. When she had time.

But time was in short supply, not least because the house had changed in her absence. It really wasn't the same. Dad had checked it every week. So she knew it hadn't burned down or been burgled. Nothing like that. It was intact. That wasn't the problem. It was other things.

First, it smelled damp and musty. Her mother told her that was normal when a house wasn't lived in for a while. She should leave the windows open as much as possible for a few days. The smell would soon go.

It was cold, too. These big terraced houses were designed to keep the sun out, not let it in, Meg reflected. Even in summer that showed.

Then there was Jamie's presence, and absence. What to make of it. How to cope with the memories. It wasn't easy.

15

She got on with it all as best she could, and in a few days she was reoriented and more comfortable. Then she began to look ahead, and to think about her return to work. It would have to happen. Time to look for the childminder she needed. Time to make plans.

She took a deep breath and rang the office, and spoke to Carol and Fiona. It was good to hear their voices again, and to do some catching-up.

'You'll never guess,' Carol said after the surprise was over.

'Robert's left. Can you imagine that?'

Meg was stunned. 'You're kidding?'

'No. Last Friday. He left.'

'But . . . Why?'

'We have no idea. It's all hush-hush. Secret.'

'Where's he gone?'

'We don't know that either. He just

said he'd been here long enough, and fancied a change. Thought you'd be surprised,' Carol added with satisfaction.

Surprised? That was the least of it. Meg was shocked. He must have got a better job, she thought later. That's all. Nothing sinister.

She rang him but there wasn't a dialling tone. In fact, the phone seemed dead. She rang the phone company next. The woman checked and came back on line to say, 'The service to that number has been cancelled, caller.'

'Can you tell me why, or . . . '

'Sorry. I have no further information.'

'Is there someone else who could explain?'

'I'm afraid not. Confidentiality rules prohibit the release of that sort of information.'

Meg thanked her and rang off.

Surely he hadn't moved house as well? But she could think of no other explanation. Suddenly, she felt bereft. All over again! She'd been abandoned.

How could he? she thought, blinking away the tears. Without even telling her or saying goodbye!

So much for Jenny, and her views and opinions.

She didn't give up, though. She went to see for herself. The house in Kingston Park was empty. The sign outside said 'SOLD' in enormous letters. No-one was home either side to explain it. In any case, this looked like the sort of estate where people didn't stay long enough to put down roots and get to know their neighbours. But even then she didn't give up.

The manager of the estate agent's office was guarded, polite but definitely circumspect. 'I can't give you a forwarding address,' he said.

'But I'm a friend!'

'Client confidentiality,' he muttered vaguely.

Then he relented and said, 'But I can pass on a message. If you'll let me have your name and address, and a phone number, of course, I'll tell my client you want to contact him.'

That was the best he could do, he said. Meg had to accept that. On the way home, she persuaded herself it wouldn't be long before Robert realised he had not told her where he was going.

But the days passed without any news or information. Meg was busy. She needed a car now more than ever, and she got Dad to come down to help her look for one. They bought a five-year-old Renault with a low mileage that the woman owner was tired of.

A few days later she collected the car and installed a baby seat in it.

'Now you're set,' Dad said. 'You can visit us now. Any time you want.'

'Thanks, Dad. You've been wonderful.'

'Soon, then?'

'Soon,' she agreed.

But after she had waved him off, she knew there was only one thing she wanted to do soon. That was contact Robert. He still hadn't contacted her, but that didn't deter her.

The woman in the estate agent's office looked up when Meg entered. She frowned and shook her head. Meg hesitated. She could hear the manager on the phone in the adjacent office. The woman jerked her head sideways. Meg stared at her. The woman repeated the head movement. Meg realised what she meant, nodded and turned and left.

She walked round the corner and waited. A couple of minutes later the woman appeared. She looked one way and then the other. When she saw Meg she came towards her with a big smile on her face.

'Here's what you want,' she said. 'I got this out of the file for you, but I didn't want old Fusspot in there to know.'

She handed Meg a slip of paper. It had an address in Gateshead on it.

'Thank you so much,' Meg said. 'That's really nice of you. I hope you won't get into trouble with your boss because of me?'

The woman shrugged. 'It would be

worth it,' she said.

She smiled down at James in his buggy and added, 'I haven't forgotten how hard it was trying to track down my ex. They think the baby's nothing to do with them any more, some men, don't they?'

Meg stared, wide-eyed.

'Take care,' the woman added, turning to head back to the office. 'And good luck!'

Meg was stunned for a moment. Then she smiled, chuckled and finally began to laugh. 'Come on, James,' she said. 'Let's go before she realises her mistake.'

It was an old house, set in an old terraced street. Very different to the new house on the other side of the river. Robert opened the door. They stood and stared at one another forever.

'Meg,' Robert said finally.

'Hello, Robert. Pleased to see me? Or not?'

16

Of course I'm pleased,' he mumbled, looking confused. 'But how did you . . . '

'I'll leave now if I'm not welcome,' she assured him.

He sighed, stared down at his feet for a moment and then looked up again with a weary smile. 'Come on in, Meg. Of course you're welcome. I'm just surprised, that's all.'

'Surprised? Well, so am I,' she assured him.

He nodded and motioned her to step inside. It was a small and compact house, part of a traditional modest terrace. She guessed there would be two bedrooms upstairs, as well as the two rooms and small kitchen downstairs, with the bathroom beyond the kitchen in a modern extension. No garden. Just a yard at the back.

'It's very nice,' she ventured cautiously as he led the way into what seemed to be the main living-room.

Someone had done a reasonable job of updating the interior. Lots of pine cladding from a few years back. But fresh paint and wallpaper in the hall.

'What are you doing here, Meg?'

'Looking for you. More to the point, what are you doing here, Robert? You ran out on me!' she charged with a smile.

He passed a hand over his face and gave a shrug. How tired he looked, she thought. 'Have a seat,' he told her.

They sat down in the armchairs she recognised, but that seemed too big for this small room.

'What happened?' she pressed. 'I was so looking forward to seeing you and the children again, but I got back to Newcastle to find you'd gone. And no-one seemed to know where you'd gone either.'

'How did you find me?'

'Through perseverance!'

At least that got a smile out of him. Looking at him, seeing him so tired and weary, her heart went out to him. She realised how much she had been longing to see him again. She ached to take hold of him and hug him. But she couldn't. Not unless . . . '

'You left the job, as well,' she added, keeping it detached and impersonal. 'Why?'

'It's a long story.'

'Well, let's start with Sean and Kirsty. Where are they?'

'Round at their grandparents.'

She raised an eyebrow.

'Visiting. I saw sense in the end. I couldn't do everything myself. They were right. They could help, even if I had left it a bit late.'

'Do they live in Gateshead?'

He nodded. 'Round the corner.'

That explained the move. This house wasn't a patch on the other one, but convenience had obviously come into it.

'Are the children happy here?'

He nodded. 'More or less. They miss

146

the garden, and the greenery, but it's OK here. There's a park not far away. Anyway, it's where I belong, where I came from. Liz and I both grew up round here.'

She had to know. They were rapidly running out of introductory conversation, and she wasn't much further forward. She still hadn't heard what she needed to know. She would have to be more direct.

'Was that the only reason, Robert? To be near the grandparents?'

* * *

It took him a long time to answer that one. He even refilled the electric kettle and switched it on while he worked something out in his head.

'No, Meg,' he said at last, turning to face her, looking almost defiant. 'It wasn't the only reason. The main reason, if you want to know, was that I had to get away from you.'

That shook her. 'Oh, Robert!' she

cried with anguish. 'Don't say that!'

'We were getting too close, Meg. It wasn't good for either of us, especially when Jamie reappeared. Correction — it wasn't good for me.'

She stared at him.

'Face it, Meg. From my point of view, it was bound to end in heartbreak. I'd got used to being on my own with the kids. Then you came on the scene. I know nothing happened between us in one sense but we were growing closer all the time. I was very happy about that, if not quite sure what to make of it.

'But when Jamie came back, and you had a baby on the way, I knew I had to get out of your life before I was overwhelmed. I had to get out for your sake, as well. You were no longer just a baby-sitter to me,' he added with a rueful smile. 'And I could no longer be a detached, uninvolved, personal adviser.'

'But the accident . . . '

'The accident changed nothing,' he

said quickly. 'You still had your own life to lead. I was in danger of becoming a nuisance, if I wasn't one already. I didn't mean to you what you meant to me. So I got out. Broke all the links.'

'New life,' he added with a shrug. 'I didn't intend us to meet again.'

★ ★ ★

The talking stopped. But it wasn't quiet. She could hear the constant drone of traffic. A dog barked somewhere nearby. In the kitchen a tap dripped. Her heart pounded.

'Robert,' she said slowly, trying to stay in control, 'did it ever occur to you that I might feel the same way about you? You and the children were never in danger of becoming a nuisance. You lit up my life! I was only happy when I was with you.'

'Oh, I would never have betrayed Jamie while he was alive, whatever he did. But after . . . All those months I spent in Great Newton? Did it never occur to you that when I came back I would be devastated to find you gone?'

He stared at her. 'Meg, what are you saying?'

'What do you think?' she cried, almost shouted, with frustration. 'You tell me, Robert!'

He took a step towards her. She saw him through tear-blurred eyes and held out a hand. He took it, and clasped it tightly. She got to her feet. Their arms went round each other. She laid her head against his chest and they hugged each other.

When she looked up at him, she was unable to see his face properly. She rubbed her eyes against his shirt to clear her vision. She saw then he was smiling tenderly at her, as if she was the most beautiful and delicate thing he had ever seen.

And then he kissed her.

'So something is possible?' he said with wonder a little later. 'I got it wrong?'

'Very.'

'You want to be with me?'

She nodded. 'More than anything.'

'There's a lot to sort out,' he suggested.

'Such as?'

'Where to live. A wedding. Persuading two fine, elderly people we can look after their grandchildren properly . . . '

'Can't wait to start,' she told him.

Screeches of delight from the front door heralded the arrival of two other people with an interest in all this.

'Meg!' Kirsty cried, rushing into the room. 'I knew it was you. I knew you would come!'

Meg laughed and stooped to hug her, and to snatch her up, the little bundle still as light as a snowflake.

'Sean!' she added, catching sight of a shy but smiling little boy in the doorway. 'You come here, as well!'

Then baby James caught up, arriving on the scene with a cry that announced he, too, was available — and hungry. Laughter all round.

'What a weight you are now!' Robert

said, going over to the buggy and picking James up.

James stopped crying. The hint of a smile appeared on his face.

'He's happy!' Kirsty chortled. 'He likes you, Daddy.'

'He does,' Kirsty insisted. 'He really likes you.'

Meg smiled. Sean chuckled.

It was going to be all right, Meg decided. Whatever it took, they would work it out.

THE END

We do hope that you have enjoyed reading this large print book.

Did you know that all of our titles are available for purchase?

We publish a wide range of high quality large print books including:
Romances, Mysteries, Classics
General Fiction
Non Fiction and Westerns

Special interest titles available in large print are:
The Little Oxford Dictionary
Music Book, Song Book
Hymn Book, Service Book

Also available from us courtesy of Oxford University Press:
Young Readers' Dictionary
(large print edition)
Young Readers' Thesaurus
(large print edition)

For further information or a free brochure, please contact us at:
Ulverscroft Large Print Books Ltd.,
The Green, Bradgate Road, Anstey,
Leicester, LE7 7FU, England.
Tel: (00 44) **0116 236 4325**
Fax: (00 44) **0116 234 0205**